ONE WEEK

ONE TROUBLE

ANEZI OKORO

Contents

1: Good News

It **was** mid-morning. Wilson sat comfortably astride the hefty fork of the big tree which had fallen half across the river. He grasped the slender bamboo stick of his fishing-line firmly while he watched the corkwood float dancing on the water. His head was poised like a mallet.

It was cool. The mid-morning breeze rustled on the rain forest leaves on both banks of the river. Twigs and dried leaves were wafted this way and that by the restless currents. An occasional forest fruit plunged 'pw-woom' into the water, setting up eddies. Otherwise, it was all quiet, the sort of atmosphere which Wilson and other young anglers prayed for but did not always get. His companions were on their favourite perches on both banks, up and down that stretch of the river. They were all observing the rules. There was no talking.

'Come on, fish!' Wilson commanded in his mind. 'Come a little closer! Smell **the** bait! **Taste** it! Open your mouth wide! Wider**! And swallow!'**

'Willie! Willie! Willie!' **someone called**.

Wilson was irritated. He **swore under his** breath, 'Who's the idiot coming to **scare** all **the** fish **away?'**

It was Ngozi, his younger **sister, panting** as she **ran,** her torn house clothes making her look **like** a wild girl, her plaited ebony black hair sticking out like twigs.

Willie, **Papa** says you should...'

'Shut up, girl!' Wilson snapped at her without looking up a second time. 'If you scare away the fish which is making for my hook, first I will fill your belly with water, then I will put this hook through your big mouth, and carry you home on this bamboo stick.'

Some of the other boys nearby joined Wilson in telling Ngozi off. The rule against talking was broken.

'Well, boys,' the unruffled Ngozi broke in, 'now that you have yourselves scared off your whales; perhaps I can go ahead and give Willie Papa's message. After that you can do what you like with yourselves.' 'This little sister of yours is too cheeky,' one of the boys observed.

Cheeky?' Wilson asked. 'I would call her mad.'

Thank you very much, Big Head,' Ngozi went on, unafraid. 'Now, Papa says you should come home at once because a court messenger or something is looking for you. That's all. I am going back, and when I **reach** home, I'll tell Papa what horrible things you and your rude friends have been saying."

'Hei, Willie, what did you do?' one of the boys asked.

'Nothing. Certainly nothing that **calls** for a court messenger's visit. I am sure Ngozi got Papa wrong."

'Nothing? How can a court messenger come for you if you have done nothing wrong?' his friend pressed him.

Court messenger, Ngozi said, not policeman, you fool,' Wilson snapped.

'What's the difference?'

'Ask me another,' Wilson answered acidly, and then went on: 'Well, how many of you want to join *my* friend Ijoma in coming to witness my arrest and possible execution?'

'We'll come, whatever it is,' someone offered. 'I'm sure you are not going to be arrested.'

Ijoma and some others refused to go with Wilson. That did not worry Wilson. When they reached home, his first comment was a big laugh, 'Ha! Ijoma should be here to see this. The person he thought had come to arrest me is not even a court messenger. He is the postman!'

'But the postman does not normally bring letters to your house, does he?' one of the boys whispered to him. "The headmaster used to go to collect letters for the village every two weeks.'

'This may be different.'

Wilson was pretending to be calm. But really he was very excited. Was this the news he had been waiting for?

'Good morning, sir,' he greeted the khaki-clad postman.

'Good morning, my son. I have brought a telegram for you. Your father has it. The postmaster says you should sign here.'

He held out a piece of reddish-brown paper from which the envelope for the telegram had been torn. Wilson took the blunt thumb-like pencil from the postman and wrote his name.

Hearing the exchange between his son and the postman, Wilson's father came out of his room. He looked grave. He handed the envelope to Wilson and stood back watching anxiously as the boy tore open the envelope and took out the telegram.

'What is it? What is it?' his father asked, moving closer. Others closed in on Wilson too.

Wilson smiled broadly, spread out the telegram and read out:

'WILSON TAGBO STOP CONGRATULATIONS STOP SUCCESSFUL IN ENTRANCE SAINT MARKS STOP LETTER FOLLOWS STOP PRINCIPAL'

I've passed the examination to go to Grammar School!' Wilson announced triumphantly for the benefit of those who did not understand telegraphic shorthand.

'Praise be to God!' Mr Tagbo shouted, throwing up his hands towards heaven. 'Praise be to Him who answers my prayers.' Then turning to Wilson and patting his head, fondly, 'Well done, my son! Well done!'

Congratulations!' the postman smiled, shaking Wilson's hand. "They call me the carrier of good news.'

'Well done, Willie. Very good,' Ngozi chirped in good-naturedly, for once forgetting to tease him.

Others joined in shaking Wilson's hand, or patting him on the back or head. Soon more and more people from the village came in to hear the great news. Wilson's father served kola nuts and palm wine to all callers. The celebration was on. The postman took his share of the kola nuts and palm wine. In addition, Wilson's father gave him a big red cock and three fat yams for being the bearer of good news. The happy postman hoisted his presents on the carrier of his ancient bicycle and rode away.

Wilson did not stay to join in the immediate merry-making. He was anxious to get back to the river.

'Papa, please keep the telegram under your pillow! We should be going back. We hadn't caught even a fish egg before we were called away by Ngozi.'

"Ah! But you can't come with us any more, Willie.' one of his friends protested. 'You are now a Grammar School student. How can you go fishing?'

'Nonsense, my friend. I will go on fishing, even if I go to England and come back.'

'Respect yourself, Willie, and leave fishing to home-bound villagers like us,' another pressed.

'Respect!' Ngozi laughed. 'So Willie has suddenly become respectable? Perhaps he will also become less unkind to his little sister. Maybe he will also stop having a big head. But even if he did all that, I don't see why he shouldn't go fishing.'

'Shut up, Ngozi! I haven't asked for your help or even for your opinion. If it came to a choice between fishing and Grammar School, I know which one I would choose. But it won't be because of your impudent opinions. If it had anything to do with you, I also know what my reaction would be.'

'There you are. You're still unkind to your little sister. Please yourself. I'm going to join Mama in the market. Do you want me to tell her of your success?'

'No. I'll do it. You won't be able to cope with her barrage of questions.'

'Big Head!' Ngozi shouted as a parting shot.

2: The Break with Home

The rest of December was spent in making all the necessary arrangements for the big day when Wilson would really leave for Grammar School. The Principal's letter had arrived. It contained all the details about school fees and pocket money, the deposit for books and the deposit for breakages. There was also a long list of uniforms and equipment, from cooking and eating utensils to games and gardening clothes.

Mr Tagbo bought them all. He was tremendously proud of his son. He was going to *show* his boy *that* he was happy. For Christmas he made Wilson a jacket and a pair of shorts of very expensive material, a white shirt and a cap to match the suit, and bought him a pair of brown shoes. Lennards shoes were the craze, and Wilson's shoes were Lennards. His father was determined to make him look special at Christmas.

Mr Tagbo was not alone in making a celebrity of Wilson, His mother began to regard him with something approaching awe. But her reaction was tinged with a mother's protective instinct. She had a gnawing feeling that Wilson was far too young to go to boarding school. Most of the younger children in the family, brothers, sisters and cousins, thought it would be a mark of respect to call him 'Brother' instead of Wilson. Even outsiders came in to make the acquaintance of the clever boy. Only Ngozi resisted idolising Wilson. Their rivalry was as old as she was. In truth, she was as proud of his success as the others, but did not see why she should call him 'Brother' instead of Willie.

At last Wilson's Christmas came and passed. It was indeed Wilson's Christmas. For the first time, Christmas activities which normally revolved around the twin centres of the Church compound and the adjacent village market had three centres: the Church compound, the market, and the Tagbo compound. The Christmas carol singers, the visiting dancing groups, the masquerade carnival dancers and the hordes of gay, screaming children swirled around the three centres and then fanned out to other parts of the village. Mr Tagbo entertained each group gladly and the entire Tagbo family basked in their new popularity, knowing full well to whom they owed it.

The New Year came and with it a renewed burst of merry-making. The night before, the hour-long midnight vigil had been kept in churches, in public squares and in private compounds. At the stroke of midnight, the air had gone from one end of the village to the other, by cries of 'AFO GBARA AKA **NABA** ...o ('May the old year go away empty-handed!'), and 'HAPPY NEW **YEAR!'**

Soon after, the long-awaited day came for Wilson to leave home for the great St Mark's Grammar School, at Amaedo. For his mother, the day came too soon, far too soon. Reluctantly she prepared for his leaving. She packed large quantities of every conceivable article of food, cooked, half-cooked and raw. She added clothes, blankets and everything she imagined would make him comfortable at school.

The night before, the Catechist had come in to assist with family prayers for Wilson's safe journey to, and his success in, his new school.

The fateful day started at five o'clock with more prayers, this time conducted by Mr Tagbo. The first hint of trouble was when he noticed that his wife was not making the necessary responses. For some time he continued with the children and others making up for his wife's silence. Then: 'Are you asleep, Salome?' he asked.

There was no answer.

'This is a silly thing to do in the presence of the children, Salome. How can they learn the wholesome habit of praying or have faith in prayers when you sleep through them?
Wake up, woman!'

He shook her by the shoulders, dropping the prayer book as he did so.

'Leave me alone, Papa Willie, I am not sleeping,' she pleaded in a thick voice which gave away the fact that she had been crying.

Leave you alone? What d'you mean, Salome? Are you...'

'Just what I said, Papa Willie. Leave me alone. I don't want my son to go to that school. Not this year. He is too young, and too small, far too small to survive there. I had a bad dream last night. I don't want him to go.'

"That's nonsense, woman. Willie is my first son, my pride, my heir. I am not ready to disgrace myself and the family by submitting to a weak woman's fear-induced dreams, and keeping my son away from a renowned school.'

'But I didn't say he shouldn't ever go. Not just yet, I said. He's too young.

'Nonsense. He is already out of your womb. You can't put him back there. He is twelve years old and must go to St Mark's. And this year too. Today, in fact. Finish!... And now, Oh Lord, having brought us safely to the beginning of another day, lead us through the same with thy mighty hand...

The rest of the prayers went without a hitch. The next clash came when Wilson's luggage was assembled. Mr Tagbo had packed what he considered would be adequate in one wooden box and one plywood packing case. But the mountain of luggage, mainly food, which his wife had gathered startled him.

'Are we all going with Willie to live in St Mark's?' he asked his wife.

'Why?' she countered.

'Because there is enough food down there to support *a* whole family for months!"

"The boy must eat there. Mustn't he? He is not going to remain hungry on top of all the troubles there, is **he?'**

'Agreed. But he is not going there only to eat. He is going to learn.

How long d'you think all that food is going to last anyway?'

'A few weeks maybe,' she said.

A few years I should say, if Willie eats like a normal human being.

'Please, Papa Willie, let us not quarrel over this. You insisted on the boy going there. I gave in. Please do not insist also on his starving there.'

'Mama, I think Papa is right,' Wilson broke in. "The first term will last only thirteen weeks. What you have packed is too much. I am sure that other students will call me all sorts of names if I arrive there loaded like a food contractor.'

'But, Willie, wouldn't it be better to have too much than too little?' Ngozi asked, feeling very much for her brother. 'After all, you are bound to make friends who will help you eat up the food.'

'That's very kind of you, Ngozi, but I've had experience of 'food friends', and I'd hate to repeat that experience in the Grammar School.'

'**Just as** you like, Willie. But remember you won't have me there to fuss over you,' Ngozi answered, turning away.

The trimming of the food packages, the unpacking, reduction and repacking went on for nearly an hour. That done, the travelling party was ready to set off. It was five miles from the village to the motor road. Everyone had to walk these five miles. Everyone, that is, except the young hero, Wilson. His father was to take him on his bicycle.

The village gathered as the journey was about to start. Everyone wanted to have one more glimpse of the bright boy of the village before he left for the celebrated Grammar School. All Wilson's fishing, trapping and playing companions were there to see him off.

'Safe journey Willie-o!'

'Go well-o!'

'Bye bye-o!'

'Don't forget us-o!'

'Write to us-o!'

'Don't forget to come home during the holidays-o!'

'Be a good boy-o!'

'Don't disgrace us-o!'

'Always remember God-o!'

Each person had a message or a word of advice to give, and for each message or advice, Wilson had *a* cheerful 'Thank you-o!' as they moved further and further down the road.

The accompanying crowd began to thin down and by the time the travelling party was near the village border, only members of the family and a few staunch friends were left, mainly those carrying the loads. The younger members of the family began to withdraw on the orders of Mr Tagbo himself. Some children sulked and clung to Wilson's hand. He bent down and whispered something to them. A promise it must have been for the little ones let Wilson go and began skipping back merrily as if they were delighted to see him go. Then began a long-drawn-out exchange of 'Bye bye-o's' between the retreating children and Wilson. For as long as they could see him, they kept up their chant of 'Bye bye-o'. For as long as he could hear their piping voices, Wilson returned their calls.

Mrs Tagbo had not said much since the party left home. She carried one of the food packages, and did not even turn to watch the retreat of the little children. Mr Tagbo had given up riding the bicycle and giving Wilson a lift. He handed over the bicycle to one of the bigger boys to push while he walked beside his son, proud and happy.

The merciless January sun beat down on them through a clear cloudless sky. They stopped briefly at a sparkling brook to cool their baked feet and to drink. They got to the road only to see a tear pass, raising a cloud of dust from the untarred big lorry road. The loads were put down, and everyone sat in the thatched shelter by the roadside. On the opposite side of the road where there was a small cluster of houses, a loudly-painted notice-board announced:

ROADSIDE HOTEL AND BAR

EAT DRINK AND BE MERRY

WHILE YOU WAIT

WHY HURRY?

Next to the notice-board was a low, thatched shanty shed full of people drinking merrily and showing no signs of waiting for a lorry or even of wanting to travel. They looked more like habitual palm wine drinkers than anxious travellers. Who knows how many genuine travellers, lured into that place, had missed lorry after lorry under the influence *of* drink?

'Do we wait on this side or the other, Papa?' Wilson asked.

"This side,' Mr Tagbo answered firmly. 'We are going up the road, not down.'

After some time, it looked as if all the lorries were going down the road, not up. The few which passed their way were packed. The sides and tail-boards of all the lorries bulged with loads and passengers. January was a difficult time for travelling. Schools were re-opening. Christmas holiday-makers were returning to work. Lorry owners were enjoying the New Year boom.

Mrs Tagbo asked plaintively, 'Papa Willie, do you think it is still safe for this little child to travel to Ama-edo today? Isn't it getting late?'

'I am travelling with him, Salome. So you have no need to worry. If you cannot bear waiting any longer, you may go back home. We can manage. If we get into Ama-edo late, I shall put up with a friend for the *night*.'

Oh please, let Mama stay until we leave,' Wilson pleaded.

'But I didn't say she had to go,' Mr Tagbo
protested.

Neither did I say I wanted to go,' Mrs
Tagbo grumbled. 'I only asked if it would be all
right for a little child to travel so late in the
day.'

'Salome, I realise it has been a hard day for
you, but don't make it harder... Now there's a
lorry we can take. It looks as if there'll be room
in it for us.'

'Oh no!' Mrs Tagbo gasped.

Mr Tagbo put out his hand, and the lorry,
named 'TRAVELLERS' COMFORT, lumbered
to an unsteady halt, swerving half across the
road, all its parts rattling and squeaking.

'Come on! Come on! Come on!' the lorry
conductor shouted as he sprang off the tail-
board. 'How far? How many? Any loads?'

'Ama-edo. Myself and my son. Four loads,' Mr Tagbo answered.

'Eight loads, not four,' Mrs Tagbo corrected.

So you smuggled in all those discarded loads, Salome?' Mr Tagbo demanded. 'How can a small boy arrive in a new school with eight loads? Do have mercy on your son.'

'But we can't reduce them now,' she argued. 'I don't remember which package contains what. I would hate to deprive him of something vital.'

'Hurry! Hurry! Hurry!' the conductor ordered. His orders were echoed by impatient passengers inside the lorry and emphasised by the driver who honked his horn bad-temperedly.

'I give up, Salome,' Mr Tagbo sighed, and turning to the conductor said, 'I'm sorry. Eight loads. Let's put them in and be off."

Mrs Tagbo clung to Wilson and would not let him go in spite of his repeated pleas of: 'Goodbye, Mama. I'll be alright. I'll write as soon as I get there.'

'Let the boy go, woman,' Mr Tagbo barked.

She obeyed at last. Wilson turned to his father. He waved a last 'Goodbye' to his mother, but she had turned away in tears and did not see him. She could not bear the terrible sight of the lorry moving away with her little son.

It was like swimming in dust, the two-hour journey on the rough untarred roads to Ama-edo. Comfort was the last thing any traveller had on that lorry. It shook every bone to the marrow. 'Bone-shaker' would have been a more apt name than 'Travellers' Comfort'.

When they reached the Ama-edo motor park, everyone was a dusty reddish-brown from head to foot. It was nearly four o'clock. Mr Tagbo paid the excess luggage fare. The conductor brought down the loads and Wilson and his father bade farewell to 'Travellers' Comfort'.

Then the professional carriers fell upon them. These boys had been doing brisk business all day carrying students' loads up the two miles to the hill-top site of St Mark's Grammar School. After five of the carriers had battled and bargained for Wilson's loads for nearly ten minutes, two of them won. They hoisted the loads, four per carrier, on their heads and shoulders. In a minute they were off at a quick trot. Wilson and his father had to hurry to keep them in sight. They hurried past people who must have been fellow students, some accompanied by their parents. But this was no time to stop. Those carriers moved suspiciously fast and might throw off their hirers if not watched.

At the Grammar School gate a barrier was up. A short, balding but benevolent-looking man, who introduced himself as Agrippa, was sitting by the gate.

'Your name, son?' Agrippa asked.

'Wilson Ikechukwu Tagbo, sir. First year student.' Agrippa looked quickly through a list and smiled, 'Welcome to St Mark's. Who is with you, son?'

'My father, sir.'

'Good afternoon, Mr Tagbo. What loads has Willie got?'

'Here, sir. Eight,' Wilson answered.

'Eight loads! Are you staying here all year? Won't you be going on holiday, son? The boys will give you names, you can be sure.'

'I warned your mother, Willie. But never mind,' Mr Tagbo said.

Wilson took the loads from the carriers and handed them over to Agrippa.

'Goodbye, Willie,' Mr Tagbo said, his hands on his son's shoulders. 'Be good. We shall come to see you on visiting days.'

'Goodbye, Papa. I will do my best. Greet everyone at home.'

Wilson passed round the barrier. The break was complete.

3: Next to the Commandments

Wilson had seen St Mark's when he came for the entrance examination in October. The layout still looked as impressive to him as it had then. The extensive grounds covered with Bahama grass, a little browned now by the dry season, the dormitories, the playing fields, the office block, the classrooms, the staff quarters all looked pretty well the same.

'Son, don't stand gazing at the school as if you were still an outsider,' Agrippa called. 'You are inside now. Take up your loads and carry them over to the dormitories. There'll be someone there to give you a bed in one of the junior rooms.'

"Thank you, sir.'

At the dormitories Wilson was met by a senior student who took him to one of the rooms.

"Who is that nice master at the gate, please?' Wilson asked.

'The tall one or the short one?'

'The short one, I should imagine.'

'Oh, it must be old Agrippa.'

'Yes, that's his name. What does he teach, please?' 'Teach? He's the school barber. He's as old as the hills. The Senior Housemaster must have asked him to wait there. Old Agrippa is a charmer, but wait until he commits one atrocity or the other on your hair!' Wilson felt somewhat lost but he saw that there were many other youngsters looking equally lost, so he introduced himself to some of them. Soon they got talking, and quickly agreed that by far their greatest need was for a bath in the stream.

Everyone would then see what everyone else looked like behind the armour of dust. They set off.

It was glorious down in the cool, clear stream. They bathed. They swam. They frolicked.

They returned to the dormitories, where the older students chattered loudly. Wilson and his friends merely watched and waited for the marvels of St Mark's to unfold.

The evening passed into the night, and the night into Sunday morning. Sunday was quiet, with church services morning and evening. Monday was still subdued. Some students had arrived late, and registration was still going on.

'When do things start?' Wilson asked one of the older students.

'Wednesday, my boy,' the senior student answered. 'Wednesday is the day. The days of grace end tomorrow. On Wednesday classes start in earnest, and the Senior Prefect reads out what we call "The Commandments" received from the Principal. You new boys will be placed in your respective houses, and the year then really starts with a bang."

How right the senior student was! On Wednesday, classes started after prayers at eight o'clock. They ended at half-past eleven for the midday break. The next one and a half hours were taken up by the cooking and eating of lunch, the first main meal of the day.

Like everything else in St Mark's, lunch was taken at speed. From the singing of grace to the ringing of the bell for the end of lunch was exactly twenty minutes. Then the Senior Prefect, Asiegbu Eze, mounted his high stool at the south end of the dining hall. He pounded the table with his gavel for utter silence and complete attention. The tumblers and enamel drinking-cups were laid down hurriedly. The last furtive clatter of knives, forks and spoons died down. Silence reigned, broken only by a few sniffs and pants, inevitable reactions to hot peppery food on a hot January afternoon.

All eyes were fixed on the tall, stern figure of Asiegbu Eze, the law-giver, on his high perch.

'Listen carefully. For the benefit of the new boys in particular, and also as a reminder to the older students, these are the rules or, as we term them, the 'Don'ts' of this compound. The 'Don'ts' are given in order from the rising bell until bedtime. This makes them easy to remember and, we hope, easy to observe.

'Here we go:

'Don't leave your bed later than one minute after the rising bell *at* 6 a.m.

'Don't be found in your dormitory after 6.05a.m.

'Don't arrive at your morning work site later than 6.10 a.m.

'Don't leave your morning work site earlier than 7.15 a.m.

'Don't do any cooking after your morning bath. Only fresh fruit is allowed for breakfast.

'Don't be found in the dormitory after the first school bell at 7.50 a.m.

'Don't loiter in the classrooms after morning **classes** at 11.30 a.m.

'Don't linger in the kitchens after the lunch bell *at* 12.15 p.m.

'Don't start eating your lunch until after the singing of grace *at* 12.20 p.m.

Don't eat after the bell for end of lunch *at* 12.40 p.m.

'Don't linger in the kitchens with the washing up after the first bell for rest *at* 12.55 p.m.

'Don't be found outside your bed after the second bell for rest at 1 p.m.

'Don't read or talk or move about during rest. 'Don't be found on your bed one minute *after* the bell for end of rest at 1.45 p.m.

'Don't be found in the dormitory after the first bell for afternoon classes at 1.55 p.m.

'Don't loiter in the classroom after afternoon classes at 4.30 p.m.

'Don't bring any textbooks into the dormitory after afternoon classes.

'Don't be found in the dormitories between 4.45 p.m. and 6.15 p.m. During this period, you should be playing games, or cheering those playing, or working on the farm, or doing punishments.'

'Goodness gracious!' someone gasped.

The Senior Prefect continued without pause, 'Don't forget the rules for meals. They are exactly the same for supper which is from 7.20 p.m. to 7.40 p.m. as for lunch.

'Don't be found in the dormitories after the bell for prep at 7.55 p.m.

'Don't loiter in the classrooms after prayers at 9p.m.

'Don't be found outside your bed after the lights- out bell, which is at 9.30 p.m. for juniors and 10 p.m for seniors.

'Don't talk or eat or move about or read after lights-out.'

'Hear! Hear!' someone cried and a bout of chattering started.

'Quiet!' the Senior Prefect ordered, "That concludes the routine 'Don'ts' for your guidance from the rising bell to the lights-out bell. You will find copies posted on all house notice boards. You, I will do well to memorise them, digest them, absorb them, and keep them in your heart next to the Ten Commandments.'

There was a momentary resumption of the chattering.

'Now listen even more carefully to the more general 'Don'ts', designed to knock the cruder village elements out of you and mould you into proper Grammar School shape.

'Don't disobey or argue with any official, be he prefect, student-police, room headboy, or work party headboy, or with any senior student.

'Don't tell any untruths, half-truths or confabulations.

'Don't pilfer, pinch or plunder.

'Don't walk about with a chewing-stick in your mouth, or exhibit any untidiness of your person, your clothes or your other possessions.

'Don't deface, damage, destroy or dig up any property belonging to the School.

'Don't leave the School premises without written permission from the Senior Housemaster, your Housemaster or the Senior Prefect.

'Don't return to the premises from Sunday outing later than 4.45 p.m. on Sundays, in time for the after- noon service at 5pm

'Don't invite into the premises anyone other than your parents or guardians without written permission from the Senior Housemaster.

'Don't say or do anything in town which is likely to bring the name of the School into disrepute.

'Don't say or do anything during the holidays which is likely to bring the name of the School into disrepute.

That concludes the general 'Don'ts' for your guidance *at all* times. As time goes on, you will learn from the Principal and Masters other 'Don'ts' for the school in general and *for* the classrooms in particular. There will also be 'Don'ts' for games, for gardening, for farming and for other extracurricular activities. 'Finally, one more word to the new boys. At 4.30 p.m. today, they must gather here in this hall to be *placed* in their respective houses. That will be all.'

"Thank God!' one of the new boys sighed. At last one thing that we *may* do in this camp of 'don'ts.'

'Sh-sh, you brat,' an older student cautioned.

'And now,' the Senior Prefect demanded, 'who was the boy who interrupted me with impudent cries of "Hear! Hear!"?'

'It was Alexander Nwosu of Nile House, sir,' a student-police answered.

'Well, Alexander Nwosu,' the Senior Prefect declared, 'since you were determined to be the first person to receive my punishment this term, write out "I must always listen to the Senior Prefect in perfect silence" one hundred times and show it to your House Prefect before six o'clock this evening.'

Benches crashed and scraped and dishes clattered in the stampede to the kitchens to do the washing-up in the few minutes left before rest-time.

The ceremony of placing the new boys in the houses was both entertaining and charged with the accustomed excitement of inter-house contests. It was consequently very well attended. The tables in the middle of the dining-room were moved out. The new boys were put on display in the middle. The House Prefects with their official advisers (usually those who knew or claimed to know about the athletic prowess or potentiality of the new boys) stood at the end of their house dining-tables. The onlookers and unofficial advisers clustered around, hanging through windows, or crowding in arched doorways.

At the stroke of 4.45 p.m., the tall wiry figure of Asiegbu Eze mounted the high stand at the end of the hall. He rapped his gavel. The setting resembled that of an auction sale, but he was stern and not genial. He was there not to sell, but to see to an equitable distribution of whatever talent there was good, average, or poor.

'For the benefit of the new boys,' Asiegu Eze announced, 'there are four houses in the school, namely: Congo, Niger, Nile and Zambezi. The procedure is as follows: Each House Prefect in turn picks one new student. The order will be alphabetical, Congo, Niger, Nile, Zambezi in the first round, and the reverse in the second round. This sequence will be maintained in alternate rounds until the seventh. Lots will then be drawn for the two remaining students.'

After that the fun began. In spite of the clarity and precision of the Senior Prefect's plan, the picking was far from orderly. No ordinary market or auction sale could have been noisier. Even with the help of official and unofficial advisers, the prefects were not sure of what they were picking. In the end, each prefect retired with his new boys to assess what assets or liabilities he had got.

For the poor new students, it was all confusion mixed with dismay. They all had passed the entrance examination and the subsequent selection interview. They had thought that they were the brightest bunch of boys around. How was it then that on arrival, first they were received with innumerable rules as if they had come to a school for the reformation of juvenile delinquents, and now, to add insult to injury, they were being assessed for their sporting ability as though that was all that mattered at St Mark's?

It was their disquiet, after the exhaustive and exhausting very baffling and disquieting. To further aggravate questioning about their prowess in athletics and football, they were given more 'Don'ts' about their respective houses!

4: 'Soapy'

Wilson Tagbo, the boy who had sighed 'Thank God' after the Senior Prefect's marathon run of Don'ts, found himself in Zambezi House along with seven other new boys. Like them, Wilson spent his first few weeks learning the endless lessons of this strange new world. He soon made friends with Adakole Ocheibi, a dark skinny boy from Makurdi. They were next-bed neighbours in Zambezi's most junior room, shared a desk in class, and were in everything together.

'Where I come from in the Central School Umu-agu Ukwu, life is much better,' Wilson observed. "We were treated like human beings, though that was a primary school.'

'Up in Makurdi where I come from,' Adakole replied, 'we were treated like princes. My father was given presents every week for allowing me to come to school.'

'God help us in this terrible place,' Wilson prayed. 'My wise mother foresaw this.'

'God had better help us or I won't stay,' Adakole threatened. 'My father opposed my coming here, but our headmaster promised him that I would enjoy St Mark's.'

'Enjoy!' Wilson exclaimed, 'Perhaps we will if we develop a capacity for enjoying pain.'

The two young friends decided that their only insurance against punishment and undue suffering *lay* in a thorough knowledge of everything concerning the school and the dormitories. They memorised the various sets of rules and recited them to each other. They studied the layout of the compound and worked out the shortest way to and from any point.

They learnt the features, gait and footsteps of the prefects and student-police. They learnt that the House was supreme and that the greatest of crimes was any act which could cost Zambezi House a point either in games or in any of the regular or impromptu inspections of the compound by the Principal.

After the great fuss and the exaggerated importance of their new way of life in the dormitories, the new boys found the classrooms. somewhat of an anticlimax. The masters were kind and gentle, and were obviously keen on assessing the intelligence and industry of the students. Apart from strong hints on cleanliness, neatness, courtesy, honesty and general good character and deportment, there were no frightening or forbidding rules. Even the Principal, the Reverend Paul M. Badger, with his rotund figure and rolling gait looked and sounded benign and fatherly. For

Wilson and his friends the classroom became a haven. This was just as well because some boys were already beginning to wonder what they had got themselves into by passing the entrance examination to St Mark's.

Saturday morning inspection was one of the occasions the new boys had heard of, and feared. Preparation for the inspection sounded as back- breaking as working in a slave camp. What made the inspection so important? The Cleanliness Trophy, a shield awarded *at* the end of each term, was at stake. Only one point could be awarded to each house after the inspection. The point was either won or lost depending on whether or not the inspection was satisfactory in every respect. No wonder the House Prefects promised 'a fate worse than death' to anyone who caused the loss of such a point. No wonder the new boys trembled!

The boys soon discovered that preparation for the inspection began in earnest on Friday. Prep ended at a quarter past nine and everyone gathered for the house meeting and prayers in the senior room of each house.

In the senior room of Zambezi House, Wilson and Adekole perched together uneasily at the end of one of the beds. Their prefect, Nkem Eboh, strode in and took his place by the open window beside his own bed. He fanned himself with a sheaf of papers he held in his hand. It was a hot, stifling night. One student-police manned the door while the other stood at the other end of the room. Their duty was to look out for people talking or whispering or sleeping, which were all punishable offences. At half past nine, the House Prefect opened the meeting.

'Good evening, and welcome to our first house meeting of this term. For the benefit of the new boys and of the older ones who suffer from the common disease called loss of memory, otherwise forget-fulness, let me emphasise that the main purpose of this meeting is to plan our campaign for tomorrow's inspection. The point for that inspection, the first for the term and indeed for the year, *must* be won. The Principal will be particular about your personal appearance. He may pull any bed to pieces in search of dirt and dust. So please don't stick your dirty chewing-sticks under your pillow or chuck a handful of groundnuts under your blanket.'

A ripple of laughter ran through the room.

'It is no laughing matter. Such things, and worse, have been hauled from under the bedclothes in the past,' Eboh explained. "There is no more certain way of losing an inspection point. And woe betides the person who brings Zambezi such a disaster. As the saying goes, "It

were better he had a millstone around his
neck...

'And he will be flung into the sea,' the
audience completed the saying.

Eboh then went on to share out the work for
the following morning. First, he dealt with the
jobs. outside the dormitory. These outside jobs
had been shared out among the houses. Zambezi
House were responsible for the playground
behind the staff quarters, the bathrooms and
toilets and the open drain running behind these.
Inside the dormitory, there was the Zambezi
kitchen to scrub out, all the cooking and eating
utensils to wash, the food store to tidy, the
water tank to wash, the rooms, cupboards and
box-room to dust, all the brass door knobs and
plates to polish, the drying lines in front of the
rooms to wipe, the inside drains to scrub, the
pebbled enclosures to tidy and level, the dining-
tables and forms to wash, and the flower beds

by the dining-hall to tend. All that work was to be completed by half past nine with no time left for breakfast. The prefect warned that he would conduct his own preliminary inspection then to see that everything was in order. After that, everyone was to prepare himself for the Principal's formal inspection at ten.

At five minutes to ten, the electric light interrupted the prefect by blinking a warning of impending lights out' at ten, meeting or no meeting. Two hurricane lamps were lit in readiness for the completion of the proceedings.

Soon everyone knew their posting for the campaign for that all-important inspection point. Wilson and Adekole squirmed in their seats when Nkem Eboh announced that they were to report to him and his deputy in the morning for 'special duties'. They could not imagine what the special duties would be. They feared the worst.

After adding a few other announcements about the general running of Zambezi House, Eboh dealt summarily with some minor offenders. The standard punishment at that time of the year with its inevitable drought was 'three buckets of water to be shown to one of the student-police by six in the evening'. Then he closed with a short prayer:

'Oh Lord of all mercy, grant thy peace through this long night, especially to the young ones whose minds are full of doubts and fears; to those who think they know everything, but do not; to the older ones whose heads spin with pride and conceit. Grant to each, Oh Lord, according to his need, freedom from fear or from ignorance or from conceit. We ask for these and other mercies in Christ's name, Amen.'

Special duties turned out to be no worse than 'fagging' for the prefect and his deputy. Wilson and Adekole were to collect and wash their clothes, and to pick flowers for the Prefects' bedside cupboards. If that had been all, how pleasant it would have been. But the lowest of the low were not going to be let off so lightly. As Wilson and Adekole were about to set off for an easy time at the stream, one senior student *after* another came up with bundles of clothes to add to their burden. Even a student-police gave Adekole some clothes to wash for him, and student-police were not all that senior!

On their *way*, Wilson and Adekole met boys from the other houses; and the happy, if overloaded, band chatted all the way down to the stream. They exchanged stories and experiences about their respective houses. They had not yet absorbed enough of the interhouse venom to treat one another as enemies. The bond of being new boys, classmates, and fellow fags still transcended that binding them to their different houses. They were all glad not to be directly involved that morning in struggling to save the points at stake in the inspection.

Down at the stream, they set about the task of washing the clothes with zest and yet with care. Wilson had what was nearly half a bar of soap for his washing, and the others kidded him on his good luck in having so much soap while some of them bruised their fingers struggling with the tiny bits of soap they had been given. They washed each bundle of clothes separately. Then they hung the clothes, still in groups for easy identification, on clotheslines across the stream. They wanted the clothes to drain a little in order to lighten their weight on the return journey. Then, as they still had plenty of time on their hands, they went together upstream to bathe and romp in the water. They decided that the best time to get back to the compound would be just before half past nine so as to avoid being called upon to assist with any work other than tidying themselves up for the inspection. Time passed slowly, happily.

On the dot of 9.30, Nkem Eboh began his preliminary inspection. He had gone round the work sites outside the dormitory while his boys were actually at work, and satisfied himself as to their state of readiness for the Principal. He then turned indoors. When he entered the junior room, there was suppressed whispering all round. The room soon confirmed what Eboh's keen prefect's eyes had already picked up, that the two fags who had gone to do the laundry had not returned. Eboh was surprised. What could have happened to those brats? He dispatched his fleet-footed student-police to the stream to find out what the new boys were up to. Time was very short. The Principal would soon be there.

The student-police found the group of boys squabbling over the clothes, peering at faded identification marks. He soon gathered what had happened. The clothes-lines had broken while the boys were bathing. On their return, they found that all the clothes were floating downstream. The boys had recovered most of the clothes, but some had been lost. Now they could not make out which clothes belonged to whom.

The student-police came to a swift and firm decision. The boys must not return to the compound until after the Reverend Badger's inspection. After that, the prefects would deal with them. The student-police sped back to the compound and reported to Nkem Eboh and all the other House Prefects. The Prefects quickly worked out how to shuttle two small boys from room to room in the hope that the Principal would not notice that boys were missing from each house.

The Principal with the Senior Housemaster and the Senior Prefect started the outdoor inspection on time, blissfully unaware of the emergency in the dormitories.

Down at the stream, the boys huddled together in fear, wondering what the authorities would do to them. They waited for the worst. Time passed very slowly, painfully slowly.

At the end of the indoor inspection, the inspecting team moved into the dining-hall which was used as the assembly hall for the inspection. Mr Badger took the Senior Prefect's usual seat while the Senior Housemaster took a seat by his side. The Senior Prefect rang the bell for the assembly. All the students except the temporarily outlawed youngsters trooped into the hall to receive the Principal's verdict.

They did not have long to wait. The Reverend Badger began in his mild tone, 'Allowing for the hangover of the slackness and indolence of six weeks of Christmas holidays, the outdoor inspection may be considered tolerably satisfactory. In future, however, I shall expect and must insist on a much higher standard all round... Coming to the indoor inspection, Zambezi House have forfeited their inspection point today for their shocking display in their junior room. In that room, five or six dirty pieces of soap tumbled out of the first pillow I turned over. Presumably, a miserly little boy was using his pillow as a squirrel's nest. The onus is on the House Prefect to put his boys straight from the start. If this sort of disgraceful performance takes place later in the term, I shall have no option but to deduct another point from the house concerned.'

Who was the culprit? This was the question being asked by every member of Zambezi House when the Principal left the hall. It was obvious that one of those fags had shoved pieces of soap under his pillow when he found that he had been given more than enough soap to do his washing. But which one? It did not take long for Nkem Eboh to find out. Little Wilson Tagbo broke down in tears and confessed.

'Soapy Willie' quickly became the best known, the most teased and the most tormented of the new boys. Wilson Tagbo had cost Zambezi House that precious point, and 'Soapy' seemed certain to stick to him for the rest of his days in St Mark's.

5: 'Laughing-Gas'

In the comparative peace of the classroom, Form 1 got a gentle but no less exciting introduction to St. Mark's. Some subjects were new, such as Science. Others which were familiar, had acquired more high-sounding names. Arithmetic had become. Mathematics, Nature Study had become Biology, and Scripture had become Religious Knowledge. Latin was a novelty.

The first Latin primer was fun, and the new students took to the subject with great gusto. The Latin master urged them to memorise the vocabulary, to read aloud frequently, and to speak the language whenever and wherever possible. The students needed little urging. The school rang with 'amo... amas... amat... They

'Latinised' every name and every object in sight, thereby doing untold harm to the very language they sought to learn.

Science was even more fascinating. It was launched in the junior laboratory. Hunched and balding Mr Vesuvius Mac-Cookey took the students round every section of the laboratory. He was keen to emphasise that science was a real, living and practical subject.

After showing them round, he took them back to the teaching section where he had mounted a bewildering array of demonstrations. The boys sat on their high stools on the opposite side of the demonstration table, wondering what marvel they would be shown first.

'Our first experiment will be called "Walking on Water", Mr Mac-Cookey announced.

He brought out a thick glass jar containing a lump of dirty greyish chalky material in some clear fluid. He cut out a small piece of the material and lifted it deftly with the point of a knife onto a disc of white filter paper. He lowered the filter paper, gently into a large beaker half-filled with water. He smiled as he noticed some boys shifting their stools a little backwards - to safety, perhaps.

'Science is not all explosions, boys. So sit still. I won't blow off your heads. Besides, if I try to do so, mine will go first, won't it?'

Reassured, the boys made no more retreating moves.

As soon as the filter paper got wet, the astonished students saw it darting around on the water, glancing off the sides of the beaker in its agitated and disorderly excursions. The piece of chalky material remained on top of the filter paper, but was getting smaller and smaller as it spluttered and melted away. There was no smoke. As the activity lessened and the movement of the filter paper slowed down, the boys clapped as if the master had given a magic show.

'We do not clap when we perform experiments,' he told them. 'There is nothing magical about what you saw. You will be able to repeat it yourselves before long. That was just a little exhibition with sodium. Have you any questions on what you saw?'

'What is sodium, sir?'

'Sodium is an element, one of the more common ones. It is one of the elements which make up the common salt which we use for cooking. The lump we had on *that* filter paper during the experiment was a piece of sodium.

'How did it get the power to push the filter paper around, sir?'

"That's a jolly good question. The power resulted from physico-chemical reactions, the details **of** which *it* would be unfair to force into your tender heads now. At a later date, you would be better able to understand them. Who asked that second question?'

'I did, sir,' a small boy answered timidly.

'Your name, son?'

'Wilson Ikechukwu Tagbo, sir.'

'Don't worry, son. Keep on asking such searching questions. You will surely go places if you do.'

Wilson was not sure how to take the master's remarks but he felt he ought to be pleased.

Next the master lifted a spiral object like the shiny foil from a cigarette tin.

"This is a magnesium foil,' **Mr** Mac-Cookey explained. 'I shall light it and let it burn ordinarily in the air. Then I shall let it burn in the presence of another gas for comparison."

He lit the foil and, after it had burnt *for*
about half a minute, he opened the lid of a thick
cylindrical glass jar which was apparently
empty, and plunged the burning foil into the jar.
Some of the students went scampering half out
of the room with fright at the sudden burst of
scintillation in the *jar*. But apart from the
increased brightness, nothing went amiss and
the frightened students returned to their seats.

'Questions!' Mr Mac-Cookey called.

'What is magnesium, sir?'

'An element. Another element.'

'And what was in that empty jar which
made the magnesium burn with that blinding
flash, sir?'

'Now, my boy, why do you contradict
yourself? The jar was either empty or it
contained something.

Choose one.'

'It must have contained something, **sir**.'

'Correct. It contained oxygen, a gas.'

'And what is oxygen, sir?"'

'An element. Another element.'

'What! Another element, sir? Is all science full of elements, sir?'

'Not science only. All nature. The whole world is made of elements of you, me, other animals, plants, minerals, the sky, the sea, the land, the atmosphere, the lot."

'Why did the foil burn more brightly in the jar of oxygen than in the air, sir?'

'Oxygen is the element that enables anything to burn. Air contains oxygen as well as other gases which do not help the process of burning. In air, only oxygen helps the burning process. So in pure oxygen, the efficiency of burning increases. Now let's see another experiment.'

Mr Mac-Cookey titled his third experiment, 'Things are not always what they may seem."

He half-filled two large glass beakers with deep blue liquid. Then he labelled the two beakers 'A' and 'B'. Next, he rolled out an old brown bag and displayed an assortment of knives, spoons, forks, scissors, scalpels and large pins. He asked six students, three to each beaker, to take part in the experiment. He asked the first one to take out one of the knives and to dip the blade in the beaker marked 'A'. Trembling with uncertainty and the dread of the unknown, the boy did so. Little happened apart from a few bubbles of air rolling up the sides of the blade and breaking up. The other students now clustered closer. The master asked a student from the other group to take out an identical knife and to dip the blade into the beaker marked 'B'. At first, only a few bubbles rose. Then slowly, the submerged blade seemed to cloud over. A few timid students tried to nudge their way to safety. But there was no explosion. The blade now looked reddish-brown through the blue liquid. The blade in the first liquid remained unchanged except for a few tiny bubbles clinging to *it*.

The master took out both knives and held them up for all to see. The second blade showed a beautiful coppery colour, while the first kept its stainless steel shine. He asked the next pair of students to repeat the experiment using two identical silver spoons. They obtained the same result. Finally, he handed pens to the third pair of students and gave them sheets of white paper. He asked them to dip the pens in the two beakers and to print

'THINGS ARE **NOT ALWAYS** WHAT THEY MAY **SEEM**.'

The boys obeyed. The boy writing with liquid 'A' did so with ease while the one attempting to write with liquid 'B' could only make illegible wet smudges in spite of repeated efforts. The master sent the students to their laboratory stools. He revealed that liquid 'A' was good old royal blue ink, while liquid 'B' was called copper sulphate solution which was used in copper-plating. He promised to explain this in detail later in the term.

'Any questions?' Mr Mac-Cookey called.

'Please, sir...

The laboratory attendant interrupted the boy's question by calling out from a side-room, 'Excuse me, sir. A student has fainted here!'

Some students ran towards the side-room; while others ran out of the laboratory. Mr Mac-Cookey pushed *past* those who rushed towards the side-room *ahead* of him.

A boy was lying prone on the floor. He was apparently unconscious, but seemed to be laughing by fits and starts.

'Perhaps he is an epileptic, sir,' the attendant suggested.

Nonsense,' the master answered. 'Do epileptics laugh when they have a seizure? Did you see him convulse?'

'No, *sir.*'

'Or froth in the mouth?'

'No, sir.'

'Or bite his tongue?'

'No, sir.'

'Has he wet his shorts?'

'No, sir.'

'My dear fellow do you really mean that if I was not here, you could not have explained to our new students what was happening to their friend?'

'Well, sir...'

'Well what? Hand me that bottle on the table.'

The attendant did.

'Now read the label.'

'Nitrous oxide. Oh, sir, now I know. Laughing-gas!

He inhaled it.'

 'Yes, slow thinker. Laughing-gas. You virtually live in this laboratory, but you don't seem to observe anything, learn anything or know anything.'

'What is laughing-gas, sir?' one of the students asked.

'Nitrous oxide, my boy. A gas. An anaesthetic gas used in medicine and dentistry.

Apart from knocking a person out when he has inhaled a considerable amount, it produces this unconscious and uncontrollable laughing when the person is coming round.

Your friend will be alright.'

The students clapped instinctively.

'We need not move him,' the master went on. "The attendant will watch him until he comes round. Then the boy will have to explain to me how he got into this room while we were busy demonstrating those experiments. By the way, who is he?'

'It's Wilson Tagbo, sir.'

"That boy?' the master cried, disappointed. 'When he asked that question, I thought he had an inquiring mind. Now I wonder if he is just too inquisitive."

6: Fight Across 'Africa'

In Mr Dudley Obi, the birdlike Geography master's heart his subject is ranked next to religion. He was a widely travelled man. One of his hobbies which had benefited St Mark's tremendously was collecting atlases, maps, globes and other geographical illustrations in any language and of any age. Each classroom had almost a surfeit of these materials. Mr Obi had got the Principal to build a special geography room designed by him for his geographical treasures and for special lectures and demonstrations.

One of the landmarks of St Mark's was one of Mr Obi's geographical creations. It was a very large relief map of Africa which he had cast in concrete on the ground between the bookstore and the laboratories. He had put much of his energy into this work. The mountain ranges stood up to knee height. The rivers looked as if *they* would flow. Looking down the Victoria Falls almost made one giddy. The Sahara desert looked hot, dry, sandy, sunbaked and menacing.

Mr Obi said that, if he did nothing else in his life, that model would stand as his monument. His only regret was that it was not in marble.

It was to this proud 'monument' that Mr Obi took the new students one afternoon. When the class had gathered round, the master handed his long pointer to the boy nearest to him and asked him to trace the course of the river Niger. The boy was standing on the 'South Atlantic Ocean' somewhere about the Tropic of Capricorn'. He walked enthusiastically towards the West Coast, peered closely, and began intelligently, pointing correctly, 'The river Niger rises from the Futa Jalon mountains in Sierra Leone...'

He got no further. He was incensed by shouts of 'Soapy Willie', some obviously in derision, but others possibly in appreciation. Wilson mistook all for derision, went suddenly dumb, drew up the long wooden pointer in his hand, and hurled it at one of his tormentors whom he had seen clearly mouthing the offensive words. The victim, who was standing in the 'Mediterranean Sea' near the 'Bay of Tunis', instinctively fended it off. The pointer glanced off his shoulder. One end caught another boy on the eye, while the other gashed a boy's forehead, drawing blood.

The class scattered in all directions. Mr Obi stood rooted beside 'Fernando Po', gravely contemplating the wild little boy Wilson, who now stood stock-still before him.

The class regathered slowly. Mr Obi turned to attend to the injured students, and sent them straight to the school dispensary.

'And now, what do you say your name is?' he asked, turning to Wilson.

'Wilson Ikechukwu Tagbo, sir,' Wilson answered. "Thank you. I am not prepared to interrupt my precious geography lesson to deal with your case. It is a case for the Principal. If such a vile-tempered boy as you is to be retained in St Mark's the decision should be the Principal's. All I can say as a geographer and historian is that your demeanour is more in keeping with that of the palaeolithic or early Stone Age man than with the modern man.'

Wilson hung his head.

The lesson went on.

Little Wilson was certainly making his mark on St Mark's! He was once more the 'talk of the town' that afternoon. He was discussed by various groups in the dormitories, on the playing fields, and, presumably, in the staff room. Was the boy wicked or plain childish? Perhaps he was suffering from being torn away from home? The Senior Prefect had put his foot down firmly in the first week to save the boy from formal punishment for the loss of an inspection point for Zambezi House. The Science master had vented his spleen on his laboratory attendant rather than on Wilson after the laughing-gas incident. But now, what could save Wilson? Would the Principal cane him or would he decide to suspend him? Would he dismiss the boy as a stern warning to the new students? No one knew. Everything depended on 'The Badger'. At his genial best, he might confound all speculation by taking a sham throw of the wooden pointer at Wilson and then letting him off.

One person had developed other ideas about Wilson. Alexander Nwosu, the Form IV student in Nile House who had been given the first punishment of the year for shouting 'Hear! Hear!', had not taken any particular interest in Wilson after the 'Soapy' incident. Alexander had heard of the laughing-gas episode but had not connected it with Wilson. After hearing of Wilson's new predicament that afternoon, however, and tracing all three incidents to the same boy, Alexander declared, "That's a boy after my own heart! I shall seek him out, and help him.'

Wilson was returning from athletics practice, he was walking in the midst of a crowd, yet he was walking alone, his large head drooping. Alexander slipped to the boy's side, tapped him on the shoulder, and asked, 'Come, is your name Wilson Tagbo?'

The boy stiffened momentarily, and then answered, 'Yes, sir.'

'Now listen, Willie. I'm not a student-police or an informer. My name is Nwosu, Alexander Chukwuemeka Nwosu. I'm in Nile House, and in Form IV. Friends and foes alike call me Alex the Great O, short for the Great Offender. If you've not heard of me, you soon will. I'm not known as a very good boy. In my three years here, I've been in every conceivable trouble. My life has been one unbroken chain of crises but, as you can see, I'm still here. I've not been dismissed. I've not even been suspended. But name any other punishment you can think of, and I've had it: caning, grass cutting, fetching firewood, drawing water, carting sand from the stream bed, collecting pebbles, turning the smelly compost pit, washing all the plates in the dining-hall, scrubbing the dining-tables and forms, kneeling on the metal door-mat, facing the wall, standing in the sun, standing in the rain, writing Psalm 119 out any number of times, writing other impositions, having to keep my mouth shut, except for eating, for forty-eight hours, and so on. I will not bore you with details of all that the power-drunk and officious authorities have devised in a futile attempt to break me. But I'm still here.' Alexander drew breath and then continued, 'Listen, Willie, the only important question is, how good are you? I mean, how clever are you?'

'Well, I can't say. We've had nothing to go by here.

We've had no tests in class,' Wilson answered.

'You see,' Alexander resumed, 'that's my trump card for survival. I've never gone below the third position in my class in any examination. So what can anyone do to me? St Mark's is proud of its clever students and does not want to lose them. The Principal always has an eye on external exams. If you can promise me that you'll endeavour to keep among the top dogs in your class, I can give you the assurance, born of personal experience, that you will pass through this school unscathed. Forget all the nonsense being noised about that you may be suspended or dismissed from the school for hitting those boys in class this afternoon. I'm in as good a position as anyone to assess what your punishment will be.'

Wilson looked at him nervously.

'You will be caned,' said Alexander authoritatively. "That I am sure of. But that will be all. The Badger will not even enter your name in the infamous black book, not for a first offence. So you can put your mind at ease. When The Badger sends for you, look straight into those big English eyes of his, a difficult exercise at first I realise, and tell him all that happened. If by any chance, you can hold his gaze and beat him, he may even let you off. He has a grudging respect for boys who can hold his gaze. I'm one of them. One final tip for the interview, use a pillow as a bottom guard. I call it "caning-made- easy"."

"Thank you very much indeed,' was all Wilson could say, baffled by Alexander's flow of words.

'Heavens! Don't thank me. I haven't done anything for you, yet. But try not to get into any more trouble. As for nicknames, they don't kill. I *have* mine, the Great O, as I told you, and so have a host of other lively students. Call me mine, if you like. I won't take offence.'

Wilson nodded silently, still overwhelmed.

'Now one final tip about getting into trouble, Willie. If ever a student-police takes your name for one offence or the other, and you are due to be tried in the compound court, you must let me know in good time, so that I can help you prepare your defence. But, if you get punished, you should also let me know in good time, so that I can show you how to make two buckets of water pass for six, and so on. Now run off and help your group with their cooking.'

With that, Alexander the Great Offender and perhaps the greatest talker at St Mark's, vanished as suddenly as he had come.

Alexander was right. Wilson was caned, and the Reverend Badger lectured him severely for nearly half an hour, but he kept his place at St Mark's.

7: One Good Turn

The first time the new boys heard that they were to play cricket, Moses Obialo laughed loud and long. 'How ridiculous! How can grown-ups play with crickets? We played with them when we were kids, before we went to school. We tied strings round their middles and let them jump about, hop, and fly. You should have heard the shrill "k-r-r-*r*-*r*" sound of their wings. And when they were worn out we roasted and ate them. And what tasty, oily, crunchy chewing they made! But how can grown-ups do that, in a Grammar 'School of all places? It's really funny!'

Someone who knew about the game broke in: 'Stop and listen. The game of cricket has nothing to do with your delicious insects.

Cricket is a game played with bats and balls, bails and stumps, pads and gloves, and so on. It's a game that's played all over the world, and is one of the games St Mark's is proud of... because we play it so well...'

The boy went on to describe at great length the game of cricket. The youngsters listened, but under- stood little.

Their understanding grew only when the houses began to play the game with their usual competitive zeal. Each house endeavoured to put their own new students rapidly through the fundamentals of the game. The boys joined in eagerly. The bang!, bang! Cricket practices of the youngsters soon became a permanent feature of all the unofficial playgrounds around the dormitories and behind the staff quarters. For bats, any available object was used; pieces of plank, matchets, firewood, and old cricket bats if the boys were lucky. They

swung at any hard roundish objects on the
ground or in the air; pieces of stone, brick, hard
fruit or nuts.

They bowled against targets which could be hit with satisfying noise; empty tins, corrugated iron sheets, plywood boxes, buckets.

While the new students were plunging headlong into cricket, the more experienced ones were beginning the tough inter-house matches. With only two hours for each one-innings match to be played to a decision, cricket had to be an all-action affair. For batting, the slogan was 'Get on or get out!' Barracking and taunting accompanied any slow batting. Any batsman who failed to hit three consecutive balls in an over was likely to be booed.

But as important as cricket was, it was dwarfed by athletics because of the Sports Day in March when the whole province gathered to watch St Mark's, the pride of the province, display its athletic prowess. Cricket paled into insignificance in the face of the preparation for the supreme sporting event of the term.

Mr Wilkinson, the Games master, with the help of the house masters organised the athletics practices. He was a fastidious Englishman who had become so brown on the games field that you had to come close to pick him out from the crowd. He insisted on meticulously correct methods of standing, running, jumping, breathing. When, however, the students practised on their own, emphasis was switched from finesse to results. Gliding gracefully over the hurdles, for instance, mattered less to the House Prefects than breasting the tape first. Poor Mr Wilkinson winced at these ungainly performances. But the Prefects were concerned with winning points, not with model *athletes*.

It was during one of these practices that Wilson Tagbo again met his self-appointed mentor, Alexander. Nile and Zambezi were practising together that afternoon. Between long jump trials for the intermediates, Alexander came up to where the juniors were doing their press-ups in readiness for the shin-bruising low hurdles. He tapped Wilson's shoulder. The boy started, thinking it was his acid- tongued coach who had come to correct his balance again. Then he sighed, 'Oh, it's you.'

Alexander boasted, 'See, my boy, I was right. You're still here. Confounded fools who thought you would be dismissed! I hope they didn't hurt too much - The Badger's strokes, I mean. And did you remember to use that pillow?'

At that moment the coach for the juniors, who happened to be the senior student-police from Zambezi House, got up from adjusting a junior, saw Alexander, and took immediate action.

'What are you doing here, Alex the Great O? Right, for disturbing my boys during athletics practice, I'm putting down your name for the compound count. Now go back to your own practice.'

Alexander started to walk away, thought of some- thing, turned and made a face. The student-police who had been watching him reacted swiftly.

'All right, Alex, for making a face at a senior student-police engaged in the lawful execution of his duty, your name is down for a second count.'

Alexander muttered rudely, but his grunt did not carry far enough to earn him *a* third count.

On the way home after the practice, Alexander joined Wilson to give him further guidance on how to survive in St Mark's.

'Willie,' he began with his airy confidence, 'don't you mind that sniping, snivelling student-police. You'll see **how** I deal with him on

Saturday evening in the compound court. **I've** already fixed up his so- I called first count with a friend of mine, Bassey Okon. Bassey will bear witness that I was sent to the pavilion to fetch the tape for measuring distances at the long jump.'

'But was your friend actually **there**?'

'Forget it, Willie. My friend will cooperate. That's all that matters. You'll see how it works and learn from it, I hope. Now to the second count. To sew that up too, I shall need you and another boy to corroborate my story that I turned to say "I'm sorry" to the student-police, but, not hearing me well, he presumed that I made faces at him.'

Willie was silent. But Alexander demanded an immediate answer. Wilson muttered barely audibly, 'I don't know who I can get to support me.

'Oh, Willie, any of the young fellows will do. You just name one, and leave him to me. I'll talk to you with him round. You've got to learn to do these things sooner or later, you know. You simply can't afford to go up to the compound court every time and say "I did it". Otherwise, you'll spend all your time being punished. We all try to wriggle out of trouble. It doesn't cost anything to bear witness for someone. And remember, Willie, one good turn deserves another.'

8: Can the Dead Offend?

The compound court was held every other Saturday at eight o'clock. It was presided over by the house prefects by turns, with a panel of Form VI students acting as jurors.

Congo House Prefect, Tunde Adefolaju, *was* presiding that evening.

'Cour-r-r-t!' The student-police with the regimental sergeant-major voice roared as Tunde Adefolaju walked into the dining-hall which was used as the court-room. Everybody stood as the prefect took his elevated seat at the west end. His deputy acted as court clerk. The jurors sat at the Niger House dining- table to the left.

As the last stroke of eight o'clock from the giant wall clock died down, the presiding prefect banged his gavel for order. There was no oath-taking nor were there any time-consuming formalities. The compound court was no mock court of law, but a system devised to guard against school tyranny and students' inhumanity to fellow students. All the students who were to be tried had been given notice to attend. The court was open to all students, but any student misbehaving in or around the court-room was subject to summary trial for contempt of court.

'Joseph Amechi!' the clerk called the first case.

The boy walked up and stood in the middle.

'Whose case is this?' the presiding prefect asked.

'Mine, sir,' one of the student-police answered.

'Proceed!'

'Joseph Amechi, the charge is that you, on Friday the first of February, were caught eating a coconut noisily on your bed after lights out. Guilty or not guilty?'

'Guilty, sir.'

'Good boy! Straightforward case,' the presiding prefect commented. "Two buckets of water into the Congo House water-tank by 6 p.m. on Monday. The water must be shown to a student-police before it is poured into the tank. Off you go!'

Joseph bowed and walked back to his friends, ready to enjoy the rest of the evening's show.

'**Rufus** Egenti!' the clerk called.

A student-police took over.

'Rufus Egenti, the charge is that you, on Thursday the thirty-first of January did leave the school premises without permission; that you, on being challenged by a student-police in the lawful performance of his duty, did run away; that you, on being confronted subsequently with your offences did blatantly deny them; and finally that you ..."

'Enough!' the prefect barked. "Three counts will do.'

'All right, sir,' the student-police conceded. 'Rufus Egenti, guilty or not guilty?'

'Not guilty, sir.'

'Not guilty? What do you mean?' the prefect asked.

'Not guilty, sir,' the boy persisted.

'Did you leave the school premises on the day in question?' the prefect pressed on.

'Yes, sir.'

'Did you obtain written permission from anyone **before** leaving?'

*'No, **sir**.'*

'Then you *are* guilty on that count.'

*'No, **sir**.'*

"What do you mean by "No, sir"?'

'Well, sir, I did not get written permission, but I *tried* to. I made every effort to obtain permission but failed because I could not find either the Senior Housemaster or the Senior Prefect for one whole hour before I left.'

'My boy, the rule says you must obtain written permission, not attempt to obtain it. Jury?' the prefect called.

Their leader gave the 'thumbs down' sign indicating *that* they considered Rufus guilty on that count.

'Continue!' the prefect ordered the student-police. 'Thank you, sir. The second charge was that of running away when I challenged him in the lawful performance of my duty.'

'Rufus Egenti, did you run away when you were challenged by the student-police?' the prefect asked.

'No, sir.'

'What do you mean by answering "No, sir" *to* every question? Do you mean to suggest that the student-police is lying?'

'Yes, sir.'

'That's better. You have admitted something at last. Then...

A ripple of laughter spread through the courtroom. Even Rufus was smiling. The student-police was not amused. He looked glum. The prefect did not understand the laughter. He looked puzzled.

'What did I say the boy had admitted?' he asked, turning to his deputy.

"That the student-police was lying, sir," his deputy answered.

'Oh no! I am sorry about that. I was put off by the boy's habitual answer of no to every question. Now, Rufus, what do you mean by suggesting that the student-police was lying?'

I was not suggested it, it was starting a fact He was lying, sir, and I can produce two witnesses to prove it.'

'If you did not run away, Rufus,' the prefect continued, 'what did you do?'

'I **was** hurrying, sir, not running away.'

'And your witnesses can confirm that you did not run away when you were challenged?'

'Of course, they can, sir. Otherwise I would not have invited them."

'Did you invite them because they would uphold your story or because they saw that you did not run away when you were challenged by the student- police?'

'Perhaps they can answer that question better than **I**, sir.'

'Who are they?'

'Amoge Obialo of Congo House and Jackson Egenti of Nile House, sir.'

"Your own brother?'

'Well, sir, there is nothing in the rules against a brother acting as a witness. Besides, we don't have to be friendly, sir. We are twins.'

'Call them!' the prefect ordered.

The two boys appeared.

'Amoge Obialo, where were you when the student- police challenged Rufus Egenti on his return to the school premises?' the prefect asked.

'Jackson and I were in the barber's shed, sir. As soon as Rufus came in, we started hurrying to the dormitory to share the groundnuts which he had bought.'

'When did the student-police challenge him?'

'We were already half-*way* to the dormitory. I looked back. Someone was hailing us. I stopped, thinking he was a friend, but he turned out to be a *student*-police. Rufus and Jackson had walked on. They did not see the student-police, and so could not *have* been running away from him. I can call three *witnesses* who can corroborate my own story."

'No! No more witnesses, certainly not witnesses' witnesses,' the prefect groaned. 'Now, student-police, *what* do you have to say about the boy's story?'

'A fabrication, sir. I chased Rufus and caught up with him in **the** barber's shed. His twin brother was there, but not Amoge.'

'Now, Amoge, were you making up your story *in* order to save your friends?' the prefect asked.

'No, sir. I did not make it up. It happened exactly as I described *it*.'

'Someone must be lying, Amoge,' the prefect suggested.

"The student-police, sir. See, he can't produce a single witness. Rufus produced two. I offered to produce three. If the student-police is not lying, why can't he produce a single witness from the whole school?'

'I could call Agrippa the school barber, sir,' the student-police offered.

'No! Never,' the prefect refused. 'This is a school court, not a village court. Jury?' he asked, turning to them.

Their leader answered, 'These children have played havoc with the witnesses clause, but . . .' and he gave the 'thumbs up' sign to show that Rufus could be let off on that count.

'What was the third count?' the prefect asked.

'Make it snappy."

"That of denying that he left the premises, sir.

When I caught up with him in Agrippa's shed, Rufus started having a haircut. I told him he was only seeking an alibi. The haircut was unnecessary. I saw him having one the week before."

'But the boy had already admitted that he went out. How could he then turn round to deny it simply because he had started having a haircut? That needs no examination.'

'Jury?'

This time, they all gave the 'thumbs down' sign to show how guilty they felt Rufus was.

'Now, Rufus Egenti, the court finds you guilty on the first and third counts. On the first count, you are to be gated for two weeks, which means that you cannot go out of the school premises even on the official free days. On the third count, you are to draw four buckets of water from the stream and you are to pour them into the Niger House water-tank by 6 p.m. on Tuesday.'

'Next case?'

'Wilson Tagbo,' the clerk called.

A student-police jumped up. 'Wilson Tagbo, the charge is that you, on Friday the first of February did lie in bed until 7.30 a.m. in wilful contravention of four rules at the same time, namely, being in your bed later than one minute after the rising bell at 6 a.m., being found in the dormitory after 6.05 a.m., not arriving at your work site by 6.10 a.m., being absent from your work site before 7.15 a.m. Guilty or not guilty?'

'Not guilty, **sir**.'

'Not guilty, boy? Well, what is your defence? Are you going to call a squad of witnesses? Have they taught you that trick yet?'

'No, sir.'

'They haven't taught you then?'

'Someone *has,* sir.'

'How *many* witnesses are you going to call then?'

'None, **sir**.

'None?'

'Yes, *sir.'*

'Fine. Go ahead and defend yourself.'

'Thank you, sir. May I know if a defendant **is** permitted to ask the honourable judge a question?'

Yes, but I'm a prefect, not *a* judge.'

'Thank you, sir. May I know if the honourable prefect heard of the crisis which held up the morning assembly yesterday for one whole hour?

'Yes. It was reported that a student had died in his sleep.'

'Well, sir, I was that student. I still am."

The court-room went wild with laughter, and no amount of gavel-banging by the prefect or calls of 'Order! Order!' by the student-police could control it.

'But, my dear little fellow,' the prefect resumed, when the noise died down, 'it was later discovered that the dispenser who had made the report had been mistaken.'

'Mistake, sir! Was it a mistake that I came back from the dead? Would it not be more human to regard it as a miracle rather than a mistake? The student-police must be heartless to feel disappointed that the miracle of my rising from the dead occurred.'

'Please, sir,' the student-police broke in, 'the full story is as follows: The boy was found stretched out on his bed at 7.30 a.m. after we returned from morning work. It was first thought that he had over- slept. But over-sleeping by one and a half hours seemed odd. A boy touched him. Wilson felt cold and the boy raised the alarm. The dispenser was sent *for*. He said that Wilson was not breathing. He carried him to the school dispensary. By then the story had got around. It was thought that the boy was dead. The morning assembly was held up. Later, however, the dispenser caught Wilson opening one eye when he thought no one was looking. The explanation is that, when Wilson woke up too late to be able to slip out of the dormitory safely, he decided to remain in bed for the work period. When he was discovered, he decided to hold his breath and pretend to be dead.'

'May I continue my defence, sir?' Wilson asked.

'Go ahead.'

"Thank you, sir. Please ask the student-police to explain to the court how a person can hold his breath for more than one hour. Better still, let him demonstrate it for even ten minutes.'

'No, I agree he cannot do it.'

'Well, sir, it appears that my coming back from the dead has both medical and official backing. Then it must be true that I was dead. Now I am back from **the** dead. I am ready for any punishment now, sir, although I don't see how the dead can offend.'

The court-room convulsed with laughter again. The prefect banged his table.

'Is this your first appearance in this compound court, my boy?'

'Yes, sir.'

'On that ground alone, I caution and discharge you.'

'Honestly, sir?' 'Honestly, Wilson.' "Thank you, sir.'

9: Wrong Bible Quotation

'We have no outstanding athletes,' Nkem Eboh said modestly to his boys one afternoon during practice, 'and so we have to rely on mass support. Everyone must endeavour to win a point or two for Zambezi House before Sports Day, by qualifying in one event or the other. We won last year and the year before and we must win again this year.'

'But what can you make of these suckling babes in the first year?' one of the senior students asked.

'Athletes, of course, if they are to remain in Zambezi,' Nkem answered. 'Nothing is impossible with Zambezi. They just have to try.'

'Well, coaching them has been like knocking my head against a stone wall. Some of them seem to be made of jelly.'

'Don't you know how to make soft jelly hard?' Nkem asked.

'No. How?'

'Put *it* into the deep-freeze.'

'But how would that apply here?' the coach asked, bewildered.

'An ultimatum, man! Give them one. During the first week of term, we allowed the brat who caused the loss of our first inspection point to go free. Now, anyone who makes us lose any athletics point will regret having left his parents' house. Zambezi expects everyone to score points for Zambezi. And we especially expect those who have lost points before to gain them now.' Nkem Eboh glanced towards Wilson and his friends.

'Well, Adakole,' Wilson shrugged after Eboh had gone away, 'he'll have to find something else for me. I **can't** run, I can't jump. Have a look at my shins. See what those horrible low hurdles have done to them.' 'I wonder if there's anything we can do well,' Adakole said, thoughtfully.

"Think hard, Kole. We'll need to!'

Their friends in the other houses teased Wilson and Adekole endlessly when they heard that they were expected to gain athletics points for Zambezi House.

Our people only use our best athletes,' Benson Madu of Nile House said.

'What do you mean, my friend?' Henry Osondu of Niger House demanded. 'Nile is never in the athletics race. So don't publicise Nile's methods. You might as well tell us what old Agrippa's athletics plans are:'

'Of course you can say what you like, Henry, Niger is just like Zambezi, crazy for victory, and prepared to do anything to win,' said Benson accusingly.

'Well, why not? And what does your lazy house Nile do?'

'Nile is a school house, not an athletics club,' retorted Benson.

'What about our problem?' Adakole broke in.

'Do you Zambezi boys want genuine advice?' Benson asked.

'Yes, if it's sensible,' answered Wilson.

'Well,' said Benson, 'there a book in the library which might help you.'

'Really?' Wilson asked.

It's called, "How to Jump Six Feet".

'Have you read it?' Adakole asked.

'Sure.'

'And can you now jump six **feet**?'

'No.'

'Five-**six?'**

'No.'

'Five **feet?'**

'No.'

'Well then, let's forget *it*.'

They did.

All went well, until Form I ran headlong into "**The** Prophets'. This section of the scriptures was one of the corner-stones of religious instruction *at* St Mark's.

Their Religious Knowledge master, Mr Amos Edet-Effiong, sported a handle-bar moustache which made him look like an atheist. But he was deeply religious. He started early to put the new students through their paces. He questioned them about the major prophets, and the minor prophets. Their periods, their messages, their influences, their fates, all these were taught in detail. One of Mr Edet-Effiong's favourite ways of teaching was the 'echo-method'. He used it in teaching the prophets' most outstanding messages and in associating each prophet with his message.

One morning, Form 1 was ringing with Mr Edet-Effiong's 'echoes'.

'The soul that sinneth ...?'

'... it shall die!' the boys chanted.

"... that sinneth...?'

'... it shall die.'

that sinneth...?'

.. it shall die.'

'That's good. That's good,' the master enthused.. 'Now who said it... you... what's your name?'

'John Onuoha, sir.'

'Now, John, who said it?'

'Prophet Hosea, sir.'

'Good. Good, my boy. Now, what's your own name?' Mr Edet-Effiong asked, pointing to the next student.

'Henry Osondu, sir.'

'Fine. Now complete this, Henry: "Out of the belly of Shoel I cried...".

'And thou didn't hear my voice, sir,' Henry said.

'Very good, my son. Now, who said it?'

'Prophet Jonah, sir.'

'Splendid, Henry. Splendid. Next, Your name, son?

'Princewill Paris Pepple, sir.'

'Now, Princewill, who was Prophet Jonah's father?' 'I don't know, sir. He wasn't a prophet.'

'You're right. He wasn't. His name was Amittai, but forget him. Now complete this, "Woe is me! For I am lost. For I am a man of unclean lips...'

'And I dwell in the midst of a people of unclean lips, sir.'

'Yes, go on.'

'For my eyes have seen the King, sir.'

'Is that the end?'

"The Lord of hosts, sir."'

'Very good, son. Very good. Now, who said it?'

'Prophet Jeremiah, sir."

'No.'

'Prophet Isaiah then, sir,' Princewill corrected himself.

'Yes. You know your pieces, but you must know the speakers too. Next, Your name, son?'

126

'Wilson Tagbo, sir.'

'Now, Wilson, complete the following, "Even youths shall faint and be weary, and young men shall fall exhausted. But they who wait for the Lord shall..."

'Shall wait for**ver**, sir.'

'What?' Mr Edet-Effiong barked, his whiskers bristling with anger. 'Where did you hear such blasphemy? Come up to the front of the class.'

Wilson obeyed. He moved a few paces and then stopped. He made a move to put a book he held in his hand down on his desk.

'Stop!' Mr Edet-Effiong ordered. 'What's that book?'

"The Holy Bible, sir.'

"The Holy Bible? A very bulky one! Let me see!' Wilson had no choice. His classmates suppressed their laughter, but whispers of 'Willie again,' and 'Soapy Willie,' were audible.

The master put out his hand.

'Goodness gracious! You've got another book hidden inside your Bible. No wonder it was so bulky. No wonder you were not following what we were saying. And what's this? A book about sport! What a sinful thing to be reading during religious instruction!'

'Excuse me, sir,' one of the boys interrupted.

'Yes, my son.'

'May we know the title of the book, sir.'

Mr Edet-Effiong held the book up for the whole class to see: 'How to Jump Six Feet'.

The class roared with laughter.

'What are you all laughing about?' Mr Edet-Effiong demanded angrily. 'You should all be ashamed of your classmate instead of laughing. This is a Christian institution, and if the Reverend Badger hears of a student reading an athletics book during Religious Knowledge lessons, he will take a very serious view of the matter. But he will not hear it from me. I do not report students. What did you say your name was, boy?'

'Wilson Tagbo, sir.'

'Well, Wilson, we do not joke with religion in this school. So first you will have to write, "I must not mix religion with athletics" one hundred times and submit it to me tomorrow morning. Then you will write out the book of the Prophet Isaiah from Chapter 1 to the end, twice.'

'But, sir, that is a very long book. It has 66 chapters."

'But that is the one which matches your offence, son. The question you missed comes from Isaiah.'

When Wilson got a message that Alexander the Great O wanted to see him, he was not immediately sure what to do. He had tried to avoid Alexander recently.

'What should I do?' he asked Adakole.

'Did he say what he wanted to see you about?' Adakole asked.

'No. But I suspect he's in trouble as usual, and wants me to help him in the compound court.'

"You have enough trouble of your own, But Willie may be wanting to help *you*. You know that the Great O is a mixture of good and bad. Provided you don't let him get you into more trouble, I think you can see him. But remember that we have your imposition to write for Mr Edet-Effiong."

'Of course I remember. I won't be long.'

'Hello, stranger,' Alexander greeted Wilson. 'Haven't seen you for ages. How have you been getting on?'

'Fairly well, thank you,' said Wilson carefully. But his face betrayed him.

'Hei! Any trouble, Willie? Tell me.'

'Well... Wilson smiled wanly, and then went on to tell the Great O about Mr Edet-Effiong's imposition.

'Wew! The whole book of Isaiah, twice,' echoed Alexander. 'Still, Jeremiah is a little longer. I've written them both out myself. I'm sure you'll be able to do it easily.'

'How?' asked Wilson despairingly.

'Oh Willie, there's an easy method."

"Tell me. Please!'

'Spend an evening memorising the whole book. Then you can pour it out on paper as many times as the master asks for it.'

'But that must be very difficult.'

'Not at all. If your mind doesn't wander, you can **lap** up each chapter in a few minutes. Concentration is all you need. That way, I've got large tracts of the Bible and other books into my head. Masters now don't know what portion of the Bible to punish me with. There's no way of their knowing what parts I've not memorised.'

'I'll try it then and see how far I get.'

'I'm sure you will get far, Willie. Where there is a will.. ?'

'There is a way,' Wilson completed.

Adakole did not believe in Alexander or in his methods. 'I'm sure you can't memorise the whole of the book of Isaiah, Willie,' he said.

'But Alex says it can be done. He says it needs concentration. If he can memorise large portions of the Bible, why can't I? Has he got two heads?'

'Well, try if you must.'

'I will.'

10: A Bed of Books

'One... two... three... four... five... six... seven.... eight... nine... ten. Good gracious! Eleven! Heavens! Twelve! Good Lord!' Wilson counted all twelve chimes of the tower clock.

He lifted his head from the book on the desk. His head felt heavy. His left cheek which had been resting on the book felt numb. The room was dark, pitch dark. He rubbed his eyes. They ached.

'Where am I?'

As his eyes grew used to the dark, he remembered. 'I'm in the classroom. I must have fallen asleep while I was trying to memorise the Prophet Isaiah.'

He crept towards the nearest window and peeped through a crack. Outside, it was dark, almost as dark as inside. Starlight made the trees and other land- marks dully visible. Wilson crept back to his seat. It was cold. A dog barked in the distance.

'What'll I do? If I go out, the night-watchman is bound to be after me with his matchet. If he doesn't kill me, I will be dragged to the Principal again. I'll have to stay here till morning.'

He sat back, leaning on the hard back-rest. He folded his arms, closed his eyes, and tried to sleep. Half an hour passed. Sleep did not come, only uneasy thoughts.

'What if I *try* to repeat part of the book of Isaiah which I had memorised before I fell asleep? It might **make** me go to **sleep** again."

He tried. The recitation went fairly smoothly. But sleep came no nearer. Then he remembered the old trick of counting oneself to sleep, counting numbers until one got tired and slept.

'One, two, three, four, five... four hundred and four, four hundred and five, four hundred and six...'

There was no sign of sleep. His eyelids were beginning to hurt when he shut them tight. He opened his eyes.

'Four hundred and seven, four hundred and eight... One thousand two hundred and thirty-five, one thousand two hundred and thirty-six..."

He was still awake. He began to be frightened. Shapes, ugly menacing shapes, were forming in front of him and all around. They began moving, closing in on him. He nearly cried out. A glow-worm flew near the ceiling, emitting a faint streak of pale yellow light which made one or two objects in the room vaguely visible for a brief moment.

It was getting colder. The wind, the cool February wind, whistled through the shutters, whizzed and crept in under the doors.

Wilson got up. He groped his way towards the middle of the room. It felt colder there, more lonely, more frightening. He stumbled back to his seat. It felt almost homely and comforting.

One o'clock boomed on the tower clock.

He pulled out some of his books and made a hard pillow out of them on the form. He curled up between his desk and his form, and tried to empty his mind. A shaft of cold air plunged down from the fan-light onto him.

He sat up. He took out his handkerchief, turned up his collar, and knotted the handkerchief around his neck to keep out the cold.

'Perhaps I would be warmer on the floor...
on a bed of books on the floor.'

He began to open desk tops and pull out
books, anybody's books. He laid them on the
floor between two rows of desks. He felt better,
warmer. He yawned. Sleep? He worked faster.
The bed of books was soon ready. The glow-
worm streaked past him. A thought occurred to
him. He groped his way again to his desk and
took out an empty ink bottle which he had used
for storing groundnuts for quiet chewing in
class.

'I'll catch that glow-worm, and imprison it
in this bottle. So I can use its light.'

He lay down on his bed of books. He
shivered as cold books touched the uncovered
parts of his body. But he was sheltered from the
cold air from the fan- light and the shutters.

He began again trying to count himself to
sleep.

'One, two, three... seven-eight... four-five... seven again... eight... nine... ten.. ten.. ten.. ten...'

Four o'clock struck.

Wilson woke up, startled. He felt warm now on one side of his body. But the other was frozen. He thought of the thick wall maps. Good old Mr Obi! He got up, groped his way to the wall, unhooked two maps and carried them off to his bed of books.

He lay down again. He draped the first map across his lower half. Then threw the second one over his head and upper half. He snuggled under the maps, and smiled to himself in the darkness.

"This should keep me warm and comfortable for the next two hours."

He was right. The temperature soon crept up, and he felt warm. But sleep refused to return. The time dragged. At least he was warmer.

The glow-worm again flew by and this time settled on the desk by his head. He drew himself up from under the wall maps and quickly covered the glow. worm with the upturned ink-bottle. Somehow, the imprisoned glow-worm seemed like a companion in the darkness.

Five o'clock.

Cocks were now crowing here and there, 'kow-ko-ro-kow! kow-ko-row-kow!'

Wilson heaved a sigh of relief.

More cocks crowed. Partridges called. Early sounds floated up from the village. Wilson smiled. His mouth was sour. His throat was dry. His eyes were heavy. But the end was in sight.

Shafts of dull light were coming in through the fan-lights. Wilson looked around him and was shocked by what he saw. The maps and books on the floor. The desks untidily open.

He hung up the maps. Then he began pushing books into the desks, any desks. It was impossible to say which book came from where.

Now, time passed so slowly, in passing before, it seemed to be running out. He had to hurry. He could hear sounds of movement in the nearby dormitories. Soon it would be six o'clock, glorious heavenly six o'clock and freedom.

The six o'clock chimes cheered but chilled him. What would happen now? He peeped through the cracks in the shutters and saw students pouring out of the dormitories. Some of them were coming towards the classrooms. His heart jumped into his mouth.

'How do I get out of this? How do I get out of this?' Wilson was in a panic. 'What shall I say?'

Click! The key turned in one of the doors. Wilson hid behind a cupboard. The door swung open. A student came in and walked across to open the shutters. Wilson bent down and tiptoed out through the door. The student did not see him.

But there right in front of him was the senior student in charge of the classroom block group.

"Where are you coming from, boy?' he asked.

'From here, sir,' Wilson answered vaguely.

'You slept in there you mean. You slept in your classroom?'

'No, sir.'

'How did you get in there then?'

'Through the door, sir.'

'But you're not wearing morning work-clothes, boy. That's your school uniform.'

'Yes, sir. I slept in it, sir, in the dormitory, I mean. I was too tired to change last night, and I hurried here this morning to rescue my glow-worm which I left here last night.'

'Where is the glow-worm?'

'Here it is, sir,' Wilson answered, producing the ink-bottle from his pocket.

The senior student looked at the glow-worm through the side of the bottle.

'Interesting. But what are you doing with a glow- worm, my boy?'

'I intend to study the glow-worm in biology, sir.' 'Are you interested in biology?'

'Yes, sir.'

The boy who had been opening the doors and windows came out. 'Good morning, sir,' he greeted the senior student.

'Morning. Did you see this boy when you came in here?'

'No, sir.'

'Well, I suspect that he slept in the classroom.'

'No, *sir*, I did not,' Wilson protested. 'I have shown you the glow-worm which I came to take. I crept in behind this person as he unlocked the first door, picked up the bottle where I had left it, and was coming out when I bumped into you, sir.'

'But, my boy, I **was** following this chap all the way from the dormitory, and I did not see you walking behind him. You're not a ghost are you?'

'No, sir, but I am very small as you can see. You probably overlooked me.

'Well, I won't waste any more time on you. I can't cope with your wit or with your sharp tongue so early in the morning.'

'Yes, sir.'

'Which work party do you belong to?'

"The sanitary party, sir.'

"Then run off before the sanitary party headman scalps you. You know what he's like, don't you?'

'I do, sir.'

'What did you say your name was?'

'Wilson Tagbo, sir, of Zambezi House.'

'Wilson Tagbo? The little fellow who does all sorts of funny things?'

Wilson looked him straight in the face and said nothing.

11: Riding a Bull

The preparation for the great Sports Day went on according to the schedule worked out by Mr Wilkinson the games master. When the heats and semifinals had been run off, it became clear that it was going to be a neck and neck race between Niger and Zambezi.

The cross-country race was run before the final day. As usual, it caused a great stir in town, the competitors drawing a long train of admiring followers, especially children. The cross-country race was a high-scoring event because it was a gruelling one. It was won by Niger House and this gave them a four point lead over Zambezi. Niger was delighted. Such a lead could become decisive if things got tight on the final day. Zambezi could not, as in the two previous years, cruise into the final day bustling with confidence. Zambezi looked more like challengers than defending champions.

The long-expected Saturday dawned bright and promising. The compound was given a quick but thorough going over. The Principal's regular Saturday inspection was waived because of the sports meeting.

Spectators from the town and groups from schools and colleges in the district began to arrive early. A number of students from the Women's Teacher Training College usually helped to run the recovery shed where exhausted athletes were resuscitated with cold water, fruit or fruit drinks, and kind words. Students from rival secondary schools came not only to enjoy St Mark's Sports Day but also to assess their opponents before the annual inter-school meeting The Salvation Army and the Police bands played in alternate years. This year it was the turn of the Salvation Army. They strummed in at about eight o'clock, accompanied as usual by their bonnetted girls.

Mr Wilkinson was in sparkling form. This was his *day*. In his short-sleeved white shirt, white shorts and white plimsolls, he was radiant with enthusiasm. First he spoke to the competitors about the lofty ideals of the competition. Then he made them fall in, in houses. Each competitor wore a vest of his house colour and white shorts. In front of each column marched one of the juniors bearing a banner - green for Congo, blue for Niger, red for Nile and yellow for Zambezi.

Zambezi was led by, of all people, Wilson Tagbo. Wilson had, by the skin of his teeth, qualified for the finals in one event, and had scored for his house a golden point. This point was gained in throwing the cricket ball, an event for which his practice in throwing stones at high fruit-trees and at birds in flight had prepared him.

The field was pulsating with the music of the Salvation Army band as the competitors marched in and were applauded by the large crowd. People stood on tiptoe and craned their necks to get a glimpse of the athletes.

The field was neatly decked with flags. There were three enclosures roofed with palm fronds, one for the special visitors on the banked west side of the field, one for the Salvation Army band at the south end, *with* the recovery shed next to it. The school flag fluttered from the flagpole in the middle of the field.

Grazing in a nearby grassed enclosure, unaware of its inevitable fate, was a brown and white humped bull. This was the traditional prize for the winners of the competition. The children and even some adults made rude remarks at the poor animal as they passed by the enclosure on their way to the field.

Guests continued to arrive. Then, just before nine o'clock the Reverend Badger announced the school hymn, which was given a thunderous rendering. Then followed a short prayer, after which he declared the meeting open.

The score-boards went up at the north and south ends of the field amidst loud cheering and the shrieks of excited youngsters. The boards proclaimed the Niger House lead of four points over Zambezi, with Nile and Congo trailing.

The first event, the intermediate 100 yards, was called. The six finalists went quickly to the starting- line. The Salvation Army band let forth with a short stirring tune, and stopped. The runners were under the starter's orders. The finishing tape was thrown across. Signals were exchanged between the starter and the track judges at the other end. The sprinters were off. Suddenly the race was over. As was expected, the winner was Peter Ndem of Nile House. What was not expected was a record time which bettered the previous school record set by a senior. Was the timing correct? How could an intermediate record be better than a senior record? Unfortunately, only one of the two stop-watches used had recorded the fantastic time, the second one having failed to stop at all. Mr Wilkinson, red with embarrassment, dashed back to his house and brought out his own stop-watch.

Meanwhile, one of the time-consuming jumps had begun, while the track events were ticked off with mounting excitement.

Back in the Zambezi camp, eyes were riveted on the score-boards. While other people worried and argued about that controversial 100 yards record, Zambezi's concern was that by winning second and third places in that race, they had cut Niger's lead down to one point. Peter Ndem's three points helped Nile House to keep their nose in front of Congo, but it posed no threat to Zambezi.

The events in the crowded programme were ticked off one after the other. Excitement swung from place to place. This time to an absorbing field event, next to a tense track event, then to the recovery shed, or to the Salvation Army band. But all the time, eager eyes wandered back to the score-boards.

As the morning wore on, the score-boards began to give the impression of two separate contests. Niger and Zambezi see-sawed in their tense struggle at the top, while Nile and Congo competed with each other, far behind.

The morning session ended with the issue of supremacy unresolved. Niger had won more first places than Zambezi, but Zambezi's relentless planning for each event ensured that they did not drop any point which they might have scored. Zambezi was in the heartening position of being five points up at the end of the morning. With the relays to come in the afternoon, Zambezi could yet hold off Niger's challenge. But Niger House was strong in field events, a good number of which were held in the hot afternoon. Zambezi were by no means safe.

The picture was no clearer in the field of individual rivalry. Nkem Eboh, the Zambezi House Prefect, was locked in a tussle for the Victor Ludorum trophy *with* two Form V students. One was Chike Kanu of the *rival* Niger House, and the other was Congo House's lone *star*, Kweku Mensah.

In the intermediate section too, after Peter Ndem's *early* flash to that controversial record in the 100 *yards*, Chima Ezuma of Niger House had been contesting every inch of the ground with him. Chima had won the intermediate 220 yards dash and the 120 yards hurdles. He had more events to come than Peter, and he also had the inspiration of his house's struggle with Zambezi to spur him on. Peter, on the other hand, was labouring with little support from Nile House. Nile was trailing fourth.

Only in the junior section was the picture clear. Little Sigismund **Jaja** of Zambezi House would almost certainly run away with the junior trophy. His closest rival during the morning session, Kwamina Bosah, had few field events to come and this was not his strength. Kwamina enjoyed running. He too was in Zambezi House, and he and Sigismund had been running together tactically in the best Zambezi tradition.

The afternoon session opened with the senior 100 yards. The favourite for this race,

Nkem Eboh, came second. It was a sweltering afternoon, and Eboh's surprise failure was the beginning of a series of freak results which made the contest even more exciting. As the afternoon wore on, Niger and Zambezi continued to battle at the top while Congo and Nile continued their inconsequential struggle at the bottom. Eboh made amends in the 440 yards which he won in record time to add to his 220 yards victory earlier in the day. But Niger made no mistake about their supremacy in the field events - the jumps and the throws. With only five events left, Niger House was once more four points ahead of Zambezi.
Zambezi appeared doomed to be dethroned after a two-year reign.

Nkem Eboh needed only one point from the pole-vault to make sure that he would not have to share the Victor Ludorum trophy with Chike Kanu. Eboh, essentially a runner, had had to struggle to qualify in the pole-vault. The demands of the coveted trophy were very exacting.

Peter Ndem and Chima Ezuma were still competing closely for the intermediate trophy. Peter was two points ahead of Chima and both of them were due to run in the 880 yards. Neither was a favourite for this event. Like Eboh, both were happier over shorter distances.

Tension was high. Even an event like throwing the cricket ball, which was only for the juniors, attracted much attention. Little Wilson Tagbo, full of Zambezi zeal, stepped out with his fellow finalists. The youngsters limbered up like the senior athletes.

Anxiety ruined Wilson's first throw which went only fifty yards. After seeing throws better than that from some of the other boys, Wilson clenched his teeth and vowed, 'I will not let Zambezi down!' He became more composed.

His other throws were up in the sixties. His best throw was good enough to win him a third place and earn Zambezi another golden point. The excitement of Wilson and his friends knew no bounds.

The next event was interesting in its own right although it had nothing to do with the athletics cup for which Niger and Zambezi were fighting. It was an invitation wrestling match between two towns, Ama-edo and Ama-dike. Each town was represented by three strapping young men with massive rippling muscles. One huge man from Ama-dike with a very hairy chest did not appear to understand the rules of the contest. As the drummers beat out their *invitation*, the bully took on and threw one after another of the Ama-edo wrestlers. The thrown *wrestlers* were glad to get on to the ground and away from him quickly. But the trouble came when they got up and tried to engage the other two Ama-dike wrestlers. The huge bully barred their way, gesticulating menacingly that they had all been thrown and so the contest was over. Despite the referee's and other people's efforts to persuade him, he ended up carrying his two team-mates, one on each shoulder, off the field, amidst a tumult of clapping, cheering, shouting, and booing.

Then attention returned to the main contest. Nkem Eboh stretched himself to win second place in the senior pole-vault. Chike Kanu was not competing in this event and so Eboh scraped through to win the Victor Ludorum trophy by only two points. Chima Ezuma picked up one point for third place in the intermediate 880 yards, while Peter Ndem was unplaced. That left Peter the winner of the intermediate trophy by one point. Sigismund Jaja's domination of the juniors had been settled earlier when Kwamina's challenge petered out.

Finally, Zambezi House, amid tumultuous roars from the crowd, beat Niger into second place in both the intermediate relay and the senior medley relay, scoring maximum points from both these high-scoring events. This enabled Zambezi to get home, painting the winners of the athletics cup by three points.

The certificates and trophies were presented by Mrs Badger, the Principal's wife. Individual prizes were not given in this competition, but the traditional prizes for a students' banquet were provided by sports-loving benefactors. One of the big commercial houses in town donated four sacks of rice, while another gave a large crate of corned beef. And then there was the big humped bull. So, in addition to the much prized cup the winning house had the materials to feast the whole school on the following day.

Mrs Badger could not hand over the bulky prizes at the ceremony, but a token cup of rice was presented. The good lady was about to present the coveted cup of rice to proud and beaming Nkem Eboh when a loud cry drew the crowd's attention towards the field. The great brown and white humped bull was charging wildy about on the field, with a boy on its back.

Who was riding a bull? Who would dare ride a bull? Little Wilson Tagbo, flying his yellow vest proudly from his left wrist, held grimly to the back of the kicking and charging bull.

'He'll get killed!' Mrs Badger cried. 'Someone must save him!'

The chase began. Round and round the field went the bull and his mount, the bull bucking and kicking, the boy perched behind the bull's hump, holding tenaciously to its neck. The pursuers followed, but no one dared to more than run behind the bull. At last a man got hold of a looped tug-of-war rope. As if the bull sensed that the game was up, as soon as the man with the rope appeared, it backed suddenly, and threw Wilson forward. The boy, his yellow vest still flying from his left wrist, landed, luckily, in the sandy long jump pitch. The angry bull, head down and horns threatening, charged at him. The man with the rope somehow managed to get it round the bull's neck with a fantastically lucky throw. The bull kicked and roared but the man hung onto the rope. Other people joined him, and together they dragged the bull back to its pen, to the accompaniment of clapping and cheering from the irrepressible Wilson and everyone on the field.

With order restored, the Principal called the people together once more. He expressed his thanks: 'to all who had contributed to make this day a success - the athletes and the officials, the visitors and the other spectators, the Salvation Army band and the Boy Scouts, the donors of the prizes, my good wife, and even the mad little bull-rider.'

Then with another thunderous rendering of the school hymn, the meeting ended. The final celebration had, however, to await the slaughtering of the humped bull.

12: What's Cooking?

'What work party are we going to have this fortnight?' Adakole asked. 'I didn't listen properly when the lists were being read out after supper.

"The farm party, I think,' replied Wilson.

'No, not the farm party again! We've worked there before. It must be a mistake.

'Maybe we worked so well the last time that the headman wants us back,' Wilson joked.

'Or so badly, he wants to torture us,' Adakole countered.

'Either way, what do we do about it? What can we do? It's our bad luck, we must accept it.'

'And pray for better luck next time I suppose,' Adakole moaned.

'Well, what else?'

There was indeed nothing the boys could do *except* wait for Monday morning.

The farm party headman, Joseph Ogbuehi, was a senior student from Congo House. As soon as the morning bell went, the boys on the farm party headed for the farm.

Joseph Ogbuehi called them together. 'Good morning, boys,' he began. 'Some of you may be *aware* of what goes on in the farm party. Those who are not soon will be. It is our duty to get the farms ready for tilling and ridging, and to prepare the manure. Previous parties have cut the bush, started the compost pit, and burnt and cleared some of the rubbish.'

Adakole and Wilson looked at each other knowingly, remembering the work they had done before with the rather blunt school matchets.

'Your set will complete the burning and clearing of the burnt areas,' Ogbuehi continued, 'turn the compost pit, and start making fences. All these are light tasks.' Several boys gasped at this description but Ogbuchi ignored them. 'Here we *go*. You, you, you and you,' he pointed rapidly at four boys, 'start clearing the burnt areas. Choose a headboy and do it properly. Understand?'

'Yes, sir.'

'You, you, and you, take on the compost pit turning. You will change over with the others next week.'

'Yes, sir.'

'You big boys, start cutting sticks for the outer fence. Okay?'

'Yes, sir.'

'And you little ones, complete the burning of the rubbish at the south end of the farm.

That's simple, but don't set yourselves on fire.
All right?'

'Yes, sir.'

'Off you go. It's already six-twenty. You
have under one hour. No lingering. No loitering.
No lazing about.'

'Not too bad **after** all,' Wilson said to
Adakole as they moved away.

'Not too bad. Rubbish burning is all right.
It's that horrible compost pit turning I was
dreading. It makes you stink like a night-soil
man.'

'Pity the ones stuck with the rotten compost
this time. But life is like that, fair today, foul
tomorrow. I say...'

'You say nothing, Willie. Remember he
said no lingering. Let's begin.'

Okay, but how do we set fire to the rubbish? We have no matches. There's no fire to take burning embers from.'

'First things first, Willie. Let's gather the rubbish together. Then we'll look for a light.'

Perhaps we'll end up making fire by knocking stones together like cavemen.'

Wilson and Adakole stopped talking and worked really hard. They were both capable of hard work when they meant to work. They gathered the rubbish and, just when the problem of lighting the heap was about to be discussed again, Joseph Ogbuehi arrived.

'Getting on well, boys?'

'Yes, sir,' they answered.

The boys looked up and were surprised to see that their headman had begun lighting the heaps they had gathered.

'Thank you, sir,' said Wilson. 'We were wondering how to get a light for our work.'

'Why thank me? I am also here to work, not only to make you work. Now look after the burning heaps and keep the fires under control. We don't want a forest fire, neither do we want you to roast your-selves. Don't forget to beat down the fires before **you *leave***. Understand*?'*

'*Yes,* sir.'

The following day, Wilson and Adakole worked as diligently as on the first day. Ugbuehi commended them, and the farm began to seem like the classroom, a peaceful place. Watching the glow of the fire, Wilson sighed, 'How wonderfully well yams would *roast* in this fire!'

Adakole made no comment.

'I think I will try it tomorrow. It will be a change from cold fruits, cold beans or cold coconuts *for* breakfast.'

'Willie.'

'What's the matter, Kole?'

'Didn't you vow not to do anything to get into trouble again?'

"Trouble? How will this bring trouble? We have already got ourselves on the right side of our headman.'

'And now you want us to *try* his wrong side?'

'Oh, he seems very considerate. He can't be as mean as the other seniors.'

'Perhaps not. The trouble with you Willie is that you always look on the bright side only. Do you intend to eat the yam here on the farm?'

'No. In the dormitory, of course, after work.'

'There you are. You forget that our headman's protection does not extend beyond the farm. You forget those horrible student-police.'

'Yes, you're right. If I can't find *a way* around those sniffing meddlesome nose-pokers, I may have to give up the idea.'

'You'd better, Willie, please.'

But Wilson did not give up the idea. The following morning, he arrived with a piece of yam. And he had been right about the fire. The yam came out nice, hard and brown after he had scraped off the burnt outer covering. He wrapped it in dry leaves and smuggled the parcel into the dormitory. There, he let the yam soak in a small bowl of flavoured oil. After bathing in the stream, Adakole and Wilson returned to the dormitory and enjoyed the yam, their first warm breakfast at St Mark's.

No one seemed to have noticed what Wilson and Adakole did that day. Their luck held out too the following day, and soon, roasted yam for breakfast seemed a normal event.

Then they began to vary their diet. They roasted yams and plantains on alternate mornings. On Wednesday morning, they extended their kindness to one of their friends, Donald Ajonwa, who seemed to have heard about their morning feast. He enjoyed it so much that he asked to be included in their plan for the next day, promising to contribute his own share. They agreed.

The next day, in place of their friend, a student- police appeared as Wilson and Adakole were enjoying their roasted plantains in the dormitory.

'What are you eating?' he demanded.

'Breakfast, man,' the unruffled Wilson answered. 'Would you like some?'

'Shut up! you can't bribe me with your illegal food.'

'Illegal? It isn't,' Wilson argued.

'It is, very much so,' the student-police insisted. 'You will need to prove it,' Wilson bluffed.

'I will indeed, in the right place, *at* the right time,' the student-police replied. 'Be informed then, Wilson Tagbo and Adakole Ocheibi, that I am taking both of you to the compound court for eating food which is illegal, and for attempting to bribe me with the said *illegal food.*'

'So *be it,*' Wilson kept up his bluff, 'but you will be sorry when you have made a fool of yourself there.' 'Be careful what you say,

Wilson Tagbo, or I will add another *charge*, *that* of insolence.'

Please feel free to add any charge or **charges,** *any* time,' said Wilson bravely.

The student-police shrugged and walked *away*, *leaving* an ebullient Wilson and a worried Adakole to finish their tasty, if illegal, breakfast.

At the proper time and place, in the compound court on Saturday evening, the student-police jumped up when the case of Wilson Tagbo and Adakole Ocheibi was called. Nkem Eboh was the presiding prefect. He looked at the two boys sternly and asked the student-police to read out the charge.

'Wilson Tagbo and Adakole Ocheibi, the charge is that you, in contravention of dormitory rules did cook and eat plantains for breakfast on the morning of Thursday the twenty-eighth of March; and *that* you, on being accosted by a student-police in the lawful execution of his duty, did attempt to bribe him by offering him some of your illegal breakfast. Wilson Tagbo, guilty or not guilty?'

'Not guilty, sir.'

'Adakole Ocheibi, guilty or not guilty?'

'Not guilty, sir.'

'Make it snappy!' Eboh ordered. 'This should not be a difficult case.

'I will, sir,' the student-police promised. "These two boys were working in the farm party, sir. There they formed the evil habit of roasting yams and plantains for breakfast while burning rubbish in the *farm* during their morning work. I received information about their illegal activities during their first week at the farm party. I set my observers on them and confirmed **the** information. On the day before 1 caught them red-handed, I sent one of their friends to share their illegal breakfast, and thus prove my case. The rest is stated in the charge, sir. I caught them eating cooked plantains and, to add to their offence, they tried to corrupt me by offering me part of their illegal meal. Their **friend** Donald Ajonwa will be my witness

'Well, Wilson, **what** do you have to say? What is it you say you are not guilty of?' Eboh asked.

'Eating a cooked breakfast, sir, and attempting to bribe the student-police with the alleged cooked breakfast. Both, sir.'

'Now, student-police, what exactly did, these boys eat?'

'Cooked plantains, sir, soaked in palm oil. Their friend will bear me witness.'

'Listen, my dear fellow, their friend or your friend or whoever you may call as witness is meant to corroborate your evidence, not to make your case for you. Go ahead and prove your case against the boys.'

'Yes, sir. These boys roasted the plantains during their morning work in the farm, smuggled the food into the dormitory and soaked it in palm oil while they went down to the stream to bathe. After they returned to the dormitory, they committed the said offence, sir.'

'Wilson?' Eboh looked sternly at the offender.

'Well, sir, if you refer to the fifth "Don't" in the set of rules read out by the Senior Prefect at the beginning of the year, you will see the following, "Don't do any cooking after your morning bath. Breakfast is fresh uncooked fruit only".'

Wilson paused.

'Go on,' Eboh ordered. 'Do you really expect me to start *digging* for a copy of the rules here and now?' 'In fairness to everyone, *sir*, I wish you would.' He paused again.

'Well then,' Eboh shrugged, 'let someone go and *get a* copy of the rules from the nearest notice-board.' A student-police dashed out, and soon came back with a copy. Eboh thumbed through the sheets and then said, 'Yes, you are perfectly correct in your quotation, but...

A burst of clapping from the court-room interrupted him. But Wilson did not smile as much.

But, Tagbo, how does that help you? Did you not eat the roasted plantains?'

'Well, sir, our defence rests on the simple premise that we did not contravene that rule. We did not cook after our morning bath. What we ate was, strictly in accordance with the rule, "fresh uncooked fruit only".

'But the plantains were roasted.'

'Our defence is that roasting, which is a mere application of heat, the same as the sun uses to ripen fruit, is not cooking.'

'Jury?' Eboh called, irritably.

'This is childish hair-splitting,' the foreman answered. "We are concerned with the spirit of the rules, not just the letter. We would be setting a dangerous precedent if we agreed with the boys that roasting in the fire was not cooking.'

'Have you anything else to say, Wilson?' Eboh demanded.

Wilson looked him straight in the face, spread out his hands palms upwards in complete resignation, and answered, 'No, sir.'

'Adakole, anything to add?'

'No, sir.'

'Student-police?' 'No, sir.'

'The jury, your verdict?'

The foreman stood up angrily, and with both hands gave the 'thumbs down' signal.

'Wilson Tagbo and Adakole Ocheibi, the court finds you both guilty. Each of you is to collect three buckets of pebbles from the stream bed and to show the buckets to the Nile House Prefect or his senior student-police by Wednesday evening. You may go."

Subdued booing from various corners of the court- room showed how unpopular the verdict was with the crowd, and, as Wilson and Adakole walked away, friends patted them sympathetically on the back.

13: Hoarding Hazards

St Mark's was busy preparing for another Saturday inspection. It was the last but one Saturday of the term. When the Zambezi box-room was opened for dusting and cleaning in readiness for the inspection, someone raised an ear-piercing cry of 'Fire! Fire! Fire!'

Work in *that* section of Zambezi House and the adjoining end of Nile House came to a standstill as students from all corners rushed to the spot. No one thought of carrying water, sand or blankets with which to fight the fire.

The boy who had opened the box-room and raised the alarm stood at the door peering into the room and sniffing the air. Others pushed and pressed from behind, trying to see round him. There were no flames *anywhere* and no smoke.

Some boys wandered back to their unfinished duties. The others looked at the cause of the alarm. The lowest shelf was broken and formed an ugly sagging V, with boxes on either side sliding down and lying askew. There was a large semi-circular burn through the wood. One of the wooden boxes was also burnt down one side. There *was* also a pool of liquid on the cement floor underneath the broken rack. On the rack directly above there was another burn mark and, in one of the boxes on that rack a charred gaping hole.

At this point, the House Prefect had to be called because the boys had no authority to open anyone's box. When the box was brought down stencilled on the side in black letters was: 'W. I. TAGBO'.

Nkem Eboh sent for Wilson, who was working in the sanitary party that morning, and was found in the large open drain at the back of the compound. He was scrubbing away merrily with a short stubby broom when the message came *that* Nkem Eboh wanted to see him. His fellow workers felt a pang of jealousy when he was called *away* from the task.

Someone called out, 'Don't be long, Willie! We're not going to do your bit for you!'

'And if you lose us another inspection point,' another threatened, 'we'll strangle you.'

Wilson did not wait to listen *to* them.

'What have you got in this box, Tagbo?' Eboh demanded when Wilson stumbled in.

'My clothes, sir... and some books... and. and some... em... a little money, sir... and some... some moth-balls to keep moths away...

'And some soap, eh?' one of the bystanders teased. 'Shut up there!' Eboh ordered, and turned once more to Wilson. 'What else, Tagbo?'

Wilson went silent.

'Open it!' Eboh ordered.

Wilson tried to push his way out of the room.

'Open it! I said. Where are you going?'

'The key, sir. It's under my pillow, sir.'

'Okay. Fetch it quickly.'

When Wilson opened his wooden box, it was seen to be true that he had had some clothes, but they were now full of untidy holes, burnt through and stained. There were also moth-balls as Wilson had said, and a couple of scarred books. Then there were new fish-hooks, and strips of magnesium foil, and pencils, and stubs of crayons, and iron filings wrapped in brown paper, and a St Christopher talisman to guard travellers, and small test tubes containing diverse fluids and assorted powders, and broken glass, and cotton wool stoppers, and two stained

and corroded coins. Wilson was truly a
compulsive hoarder.

It was clear to everyone around that some
of Wilson's test tubes had got broken, letting out
corrosive chemicals which had burnt his
clothes, his box and the wooden racks.

'Tagbo, did you steal all those articles from
the laboratory?' Eboh asked.

'I did not steal them, sir. They were left-
overs from the laboratory assistant's work. I
explained that I wanted them for science
demonstrations to my friends at home. In fact
he told me that the Science master would also
be pleased to hear of my enthusiasm, but he had
not told him.'

'Do you now want to implicate the
laboratory assistant, boy? This is a matter for
the Principal, Tagbo. Replace all those exhibits
in the box, lock it, and go back to your work.
The Principal will see you next week.'

Wilson *obeyed.*

'Hand me that *key*!' Eboh ordered.

Wilson did, and went back to his work. Some of the students followed him out. Others remained. Eboh looked ruefully at the mess. He shook his head. But his immediate problem was how to conceal the mess and destruction from the prying eyes and poking fingers of the Reverend Badger who was due before long on his tour of inspection. He did not care what the Principal did to Wilson afterwards as long as Zambezi house did not lose another inspection point.

Wilson refused to answer questions from other students. This time he was genuinely perturbed. All the other scrapes had been looked upon as signs of youthful exuberance. But this was different. He *was* dismayed by the prefect's suggestion of stealing. He was worried about the damaged rack. He knew how the Principal valued school property.

'I think I've had it at St Mark's,' he moaned to Adakole.

'But you did not set out deliberately to damage that rotten old rack,' Adakole argued.

'That's beside the point,' sighed Wilson. The damage is done. It is the removal of those silly little articles from the lab which will cause trouble.'

'But, Willie,' Adakole went on, 'the Principal might give you a hearing first. He did last time. You didn't intend to destroy school property. And surely the lab assistant will say he *gave* you the chemicals and other things.'

'But how am I going to survive the next week, the examination week, with this trouble hanging over me? I'll probably fail the examination which would give The Badger another reason to *sack* me. Remember he said that anyone who failed the first term examination would be thrown out.'

'You won't fail,' Adakole prophesied. 'So let's decide what you should say to The Badger when the time comes.'

'M-hm, what can I say? That the box-room rack was not burnt by chemicals from my box? That those chemicals and other odds and ends did not come from the lab?'

'No,' said Adakole firmly. 'You must say that the burn was accidental. That you did not intend to damage school property. That the lab assistant gave you all those odds and ends. That you did not steal them. That's the truth, and The Badger should believe you.'

'I suppose you're right. If The Badger chooses to believe that I stole, let him sack me.'

At this point, Alexander Nwosu came up behind them.

'Hello, my little friend,' he began, 'I'm very sorry to hear that your clothes and other things in your box were burnt. If you need anything to wear, don't hesitate to ask me. I can give you a couple of shirts. They'll be a little large for you at the moment, but you'll soon grow to fill them.'

Wilson was not sure whether Alexander's visit would bring him good or ill. So he was silent at first. He was surprised that Alexander was the first person to express concern about his personal loss.

'Thank you very much,' he found his voice at last. 'Everyone else talks as if I'd burnt down half the school instead of a rotten old wooden rack. They've all chosen to side with the Principal, not caring to spare a thought for me, though I've lost virtually all my earthly possessions.'

'Oh, never mind, Willie. Forget the students. You don't have to defend yourself against them, but remember you will have to face The Badger again when the report goes up. So what do you propose *to* say *to him*?"

'I suppose I have to admit everything since the exhibits are there.'

'Don't be silly, Willie. You mustn't admit every- thing *just* like that. It will depend on what the report says. If the prefect insists that you stole those articles from the lab, surely you won't be mad enough to admit that. The lab assistant gave them to you for your private experiments during the holidays, didn't *he*?'

'Of course, he did.'

'Well then, Badger should believe you. But do you know what will bowl him over completely?'

'No.'

'Well, ask him to open the boxes of all the other new students, to see for himself how many of them have collections similar to your own. If he proposes to send you away for the revelations of that unfortunate accident, he may have to consider sending away a host of other students as well. You can add that a number of older students have not grown out of the habit of picking up odds and ends from the laboratories. That should start him thinking.'

Wilson nodded, knowing that this was true.

"Coming to the question of damaging school property,' Alexander went on, you could also bring up something which should make The Badger sit up."

'What's *that*?' Wilson asked.

'We *have* already mentioned it. Give him a list of your own losses in that accident - clothes, books, money and the box itself. Tell him you now have no clothes to wear, no box to carry your remaining books in, and no money to travel home with. All that may not be strictly accurate, but when you are defending yourself, general rather than strict accuracy is what concerns you. If Badger can find an easy answer to your problem, I should be interested to know.'

'Thank you again,' Wilson said. 'You've been very helpful.'

'And now, Willie, how ready are you for next week?' Alexander asked.

'Next week? What's happening?'

'What's happening? Why, the exams of course!'

'Oh yes, I know, I'm sure this trouble will upset me then.'

'Well, it mustn't,' Alexander said firmly. 'You must hold a good position in your class. Remember what I told you. Keep among the top dogs in your class and you'll stay in the school.'

'I'll do my best,' Wilson promised.

The examinations started on Monday morning. Wilson waited to be called up by the Principal. Nothing happened.

14: Call to the Badger

When Mr Tagbo told his wife about the Principal's letter asking him to come up to St Mark's to discuss an important matter, she broke into frantic and uncontrollable wailing.

'Oh Willie, my son, my son! Oh Willie, my son is dead! Willie-o! Willie! Willie-o! Willie ...!'

She 'knew' in a flash that her son must be dead. No other thought occurred to her. Her husband, who was less fatalistic though no less disturbed, could not dissuade her from her fixed idea.

Ngozi and the other children rushed to their mother's side, fearing the worst.

'What is it, Mama? What is the matter?' Ngozi asked.

Willie-o! Willie! Ask your father-o! Willie-o! Willie! He sent my son away-o! Willie! What shall I do-o! Willie! Willie-o! Willie... !'

'Mama, has anything happened to Willie?' Ngozi asked in tears.

Yes-o! Willie! Your father said so-o! Willie...!' 'I said nothing,' Mr Tagbo declared. 'I told her that I received a letter from Willie's Principal asking me *to* come up to the school next week for an important discussion...'

The children were not listening to any long-winded explanation from their father. They fell quickly into their mother's mournful chant, 'Willie-o! Willie!' and their weeping drowned whatever their father was trying to tell the neighbours who were streaming in, alarmed by Mrs Tagbo's wailing.

... The Principal could be wanting to discuss anything under the sun,' Mr Tagbo continued. "This woman is plain silly. See how she has

dragged the children into her thoughtless
mourning. If our son was dead or even seriously
ill, the Principal would want to see me now, not
next week.'

'Has the boy been writing to you?' one of
the neighbours asked.

'He has, of course.'

'And he never said he was ill?'

'No.'

'And no one in the school wrote to say that
your boy was ill?'

'No one did.'

'Then there is no cause for alarm. Make
sure you keep the appointment, Mr Tagbo. Who
knows if the Principal is not considering your
boy for a scholarship? We all believe that the
boy is exceptional.'

Mr Tagbo tried once more to calm down his
wife. 'Now shut up, woman! Pull yourself

together *at* once. Willie is also my son, my first son. You cannot be more concerned about him than I am.

'But my son is so young-o! He is so tender... I said he should not go... I wonder why you sent him to that hard school... Perhaps they have starved him to death-o! Or killed him with hard work-o! Or perhaps... Oh God I don't know what to do...

Mr and Mrs Tagbo arrived at St Mark's on Monday morning accompanied by a number of relatives and friends. They had traveled by overnight lorry.

At the school gate, Mr and Mrs Tagbo and their sad and sullen entourage were met by Agrippa the school barber. Agrippa read Mrs Tagbo's sad and swollen face and promptly banished her fears by telling her that her son Wilson was alive and well.

"They call him "Willie-in-trouble", he added, 'because he has got into a scrape or two. The sort of things little boys get up to, you know. All the little boys here play pranks and get into trouble now and then, but there is nothing serious, really.'

"Thank you very much, sir,' Mrs Tagbo managed to say, the barest flicker of a smile crossing her pale, drawn face.

'Oh there is nothing to thank me for,' Agrippa said modestly. 'I love helping people.'

'When can I see him, sir?' Mr Tagbo asked Agrippa, treating him with deference like a member of the school staff.

"The big man? Soon,' Agrippa answered. "They are at morning prayers now, but soon the big man will return to his office. I will take you up to him soon.' Agrippa behaved with such an overwhelming air of confidence that few people ever spurned his advice or direction. He offered Mrs Tagbo and the other people the hospitality of the creaky bamboo seats in his shed I while he took Mr Tagbo aside to drop a few hints about what to say to the Principal.

'Your main interview is going to be with the Senior Housemaster because of the nature of your son's difficulties. But you must first keep your appoint- ment with the big man,' Agrippa said.

Mr Tagbo handed over his walking stick to his wife as she sat meekly in Agrippa's shed. He and Agrippa then set off for the Principal's office. Agrippa's clattering scissors gait was quick and confident, though he looked ungainly as he led the way along one side of the playing-field and up the pebbled and royal palm-lined path to the Principal's office. When Agrippa had handed over Mr Tagbo to the Principal's elderly khaki-clad office 'boy', he waddled back triumphantly to his shed, ready to entertain his visitors or to take on the next caller or the next emergency.

The interview with the Reverend Badger was brief, exactly as Agrippa had forecast. Mr Tagbo agreed to pay the cost of repairing the burnt rack in the Zambezi House box-room. He agreed it would help to drive home to his son the gravity of such damage to school property. He disagreed with the Principal's suggestion that Wilson had had an unhappy and repressed upbringing, but promised to take a more personal interest in the boy's welfare.

The Senior House Master, grumpy Mr David Oji, was less friendly.

'Morning Mr Tagbo,' he began in response to Mr Tagbo's 'Good morning, sir.' 'I'm afraid your son Wilson has given this school more headaches in one term than we are used to getting from a whole class in one year.'

I'm very sorry to hear that,' Mr Tagbo readily apologised.

You need to be more sorry than that, Mr Tagbo. Boys are usually up to some mischief now and again. We make allowance for that. But we've had very few boys who've looked for trouble as Wilson does. Since the beginning of the term, your son has had one new trouble every week..."

'One week, one trouble?' Mr Tagbo cried in utter disbelief.

'Precisely that, Mr Tagbo. The first week, he stored pieces of soap under his pillow, and cost his house a valuable inspection point. The second week, he breathed a dangerous gas in the laboratory, and nearly died...

'Please what is the laboratory?' Mr Tagbo asked.

'Oh, the place where students study science,' Mr Oji answered.

'I am sorry to have to ask all these questions, sir. But what is science?'

'Science,' the Senior House Master began uncertainly, is one of the new subjects we teach boys. It is... em... a kind of knowledge. The boys perform experiments and so on. Anyway, I am not a scientist. I teach ancient history. Anyway your boy Wilson got into trouble there during the second week,' the master continued, hurrying back to safer ground before Mr Tagbo could ask him to explain 'experiments". "The third week, he hit his classmates with a stick during Geography. The fourth week,' Mr Oji hurried on before he had to explain that word, 'he slept throughout the morning, pretending to be dead. So he went on, week after week, breaking one rule after another, until this latest occasion which led to our sending for you after your son had attempted to burn down the dormitory with dangerous chemicals which he had taken from the laboratory, that same place where he had breathed the dangerous gas.'

'I am surprised. I feel ashamed. But I used to be proud of Willie, my son before he left home."

'Well, you won't be now, Mr Tagbo. You can't. If we had not discovered him in time, it would have been your house which would have been blown up during the holidays. Your son, of whom you used to be so proud, was hoarding those dangerous chemicals to take home for fooling around with during the holidays.'

'No!' Mr Tagbo gasped.

'Yes indeed, Mr Tagbo. Yes. Now, what kind of home have you got?'

'In what way, please?'

'As far as peace and stability are concerned. Wilson's adjustment difficulties may be explained by his having had an unstable and insecure upbringing. Have you many wives, Mr Tagbo?'

'No. One only. His mother.'

'Have you always been married to her?'

'No. Only since our wedding day.'

'How many children?'

'Only seven yet. Willie is the oldest.'

'Is there any unstable or criminal trait on either side, yours or your wife's, in this generation or earlier?'

'No!' Mr Tagbo spat, angry.

'Well, I'm sorry to have asked all that, Mr Tagbo, but, when we have a boy with such difficulties as Wilson has had, it is our duty, sometimes painful and unpleasant, *to* dig into the family background for an answer, *an* explanation, or a way of helping to return such a boy to the path of rectitude.'

'True, my son has done a few crazy things in the few months he has spent in your school, but they *may* all have been genuine childish pranks. There is no history of crime and wickedness in our family. My son has always been very gentle with, and kind to, his mother. He is a good boy.' Mr Tagbo was feeling more and more defensive.

"Thank you, Mr Tagbo, for your frankness. I believe what you say. But what shall we do? We've done our best here to help your son. But it appears impossible to set him right. However, we have not given up. The Principal has decided that if the boy's school work matches his behaviour, he will have to be sent away. But if he does reasonably well in his examinations he may stay, on trial, for another term.'

Mr Tagbo was so relieved by the news that Wilson might still have a chance that he wrung Mr Oji warmly by the hand.

'Thank you very much, sir. Thank you. Would it be possible for us to see Willie before *we* go?'

'Of course. You may see him during the recess.'

"Thank you, thank you, sir.'

'Goodbye, Mr Tagbo.'

'Goodbye.'

The interview with Wilson lasted only a few minutes. Wilson met his parents in Agrippa's shed where Mr Tagbo was constrained to push his wife out of the *way* because of her doting behaviour to their son. Then he told Wilson briefly what had passed between him and the Principal and Senior House- master.

'You have been very bad, my son. I am ashamed.

And now everything hangs on your examination result,' Mr Tagbo added. 'Do you think it will be good? Did you do well, with all these troubles?'

'I don't know, Papa.' Wilson answered huskily. 'Well,' Mr Tagbo shrugged, 'we must leave everything to God. There's the bell. Go at once, or you'll get into trouble yet again. Our friend Mr Agrippa here will keep the parcels we brought for you. You can pick them up at the end of classes. I shall return on Friday to collect you and to hear the final verdict. Goodbye, Willie.'

'Goodbye, **Papa**. Goodbye, Mama. Greet Ngozi and all the other little children. Tell them I will be back on Friday.'

Wilson could hear his mother weeping quietly as he left, but he did not look back.

15: Wilson's Fate

The agony of suspense for Wilson as he waited for the exam results was somewhat camouflaged as the excitement attending inter-house matches rose to a crescendo. Each house fought for the honour of flying its pennant over the school tower during the following term. Unlike athletics, no fraternal feast followed victory in other games, and whoever won them basked alone in the sunshine of victory.

The green pennant of Congo House had been flying since January following their victory in the previous year's third term games. Congo was determined to keep that green pennant flying there, while all the other houses were determined to bring *it* down.

The first term's games were cricket, hockey and volleyball. Tunde Adefolaju, the Congo House Prefect, was also the school cricket captain. He coached his players well and infused them with his enthusiasm. Not unexpectedly both the Congo senior and intermediate teams beat all comers, although the juniors won only two of their matches.

Hockey evoked more bad blood than cricket. Matches were played like close-combat infantry charges. At hockey the fighting spirit of Zambezi House gave them a special advantage. The final match between Zambezi and Niger had been a fierce battle which Mr Wilkinson had hardly been able to control. When his final whistle had brought hostilities to an end, Zambezi were the winners of both the match and the inter-house hockey competition, but at the cost of injured players on both sides.

Zambezi students were delirious. They took over the field for a victory dance, having now established themselves as direct challengers to Congo. They all believed that they would soon replace the green flag of Congo with their yellow.

The volley-ball competition must now decide the points for the winning house. Again Zambezi and Congo were neck and neck, but Zambezi had one intermediate match against Nile House in hand. If they won this their flag would fly over the school next term.

'There's still a chance!' said Wilson excitedly to Adakole.

The volley-ball match was played on the last Wednesday of term. It was to be no ordinary inter- house affair. Everyone in the school was aware of its significance. Everyone was interested. Volley-ball had never before caused such a stir at St Mark's. In fact many people had considered it as a cissy game fit only for women. The volley-ball court was tucked away in one corner of the school compound and there was very limited space for spectators. The only real vantage point was the high ground *at* the end of Mrs Badger's chicken run. Normally few people cared enough about volley-ball to trouble themselves with climbing up there.

On that Wednesday things were different. Many students jostled to get to that high ground by the chicken run. The frail wire netting of the run was soon in danger of collapsing and the hens cackled wildly as so many people intruded on their privacy. Other students trampled down the tall succulent elephant grass on the east side of the court to create more standing room.

Just before five the teams arrived. From the cheering they received, one would have thought that they were arriving for an inter-collegiate soccer match.

Mr Wilkinson was there to umpire the match. Zambezi won the toss and chose the west side of the court. Mr Wilkinson blew his whistle for service, and the linesmen sharpened their eyes. The ball was palmed to and fro over the net for a long exchange. Then a Nile player leapt very high and smashed the ball on the head of a startled, briefly absent-minded Zambezi player for Nile's first point.

The crowd cheered as if it was the end of the game. Nile then went on to win all five points from their service. Zambezi players seemed unruffled. When it was their turn to serve, they retaliated by picking up five points from their service. After Nile had repeated the performance to run up a 10-5 lead, and Zambezi had won the first two points from their next service,

it looked as if the ding-dong battle would go on unchecked. But Nile players soon broke

Zambezi's service and attacked with furious smashes after two or three passes on their side. For a short time Nile drew ahead, but Zambezi, adaptable as ever, modified their technique to the tempo of Nile's game and pulled up from 7-15 to 15 all. Nile then pulled away again, and won the first game 21-17.

The teams changed sides. Zambezi was still in their trough when the second game started, and Nile was soon leading again, riding happily towards victory. The chance to overtake Congo House for the term's championship was slipping away from Zambezi. The Nile and Congo supporters roared Nile on.

'Revenge is sweet!' the Nile and Congo supporters crowed. 'Grind Zambezi to dust!'

Poor Zambezi did not even have the cold comfort of Niger's support. Niger was not in love with Zambezi after Zambezi's narrow win in athletics in the previous month. Again it would have called for the noblest of sporting spirits for Niger boys to be pro-Zambezi after Zambezi seniors and intermediates had also beaten Niger in both cricket and volley-ball.

But the Zambezi team spirit was a match for this sort of situation. Yet again they surged ahead and soon overtook a surprised Nile and stormed to a 6-point lead. The precision of their systematic game became more and more disconcerting to the thrustful Nile boys. Zambezi's distribution, their placing of balls, and their passing shots began to overwhelm their opponents who seemed to wilt and fold up. Zambezi won easily 21-12. Revenge was sweet indeed!

They changed sides again for the decider. The *state* of the match had been relayed by word of mouth to the dormitories. Any students left there raced to the field for the grandstand finish. The championship now hung on the slender thread of that last game. Whose stamina would outlast the other's? Nile's or Zambezi's? Congo House supporters were despondent though not silent. They felt sure that Zambezi would now swamp Nile, who actually had nothing to fight for, and snatch the coveted championship. Congo felt impotent to influence the result. All they could do was watch, cheer and pray.

But watch, cheer and pray hard as they did, Congo's fears were painfully justified by Zambezi's lead of 11-4 when the final game was only a few minutes old. Some Congo boys began to skulk away from the field, dejected and angry. Nile's final inert performance had been sickening. Some irate Congo partisans even voiced the suspicion that Nile was throwing the game away on purpose to thwart Congo. But anyone who was conscious of the unrelenting rivalry between the houses would know that Nile would not throw any game away to Zambezi of all houses. No one, other than Zambezi boys, ever wanted Zambezi to win, and if they did win, it would be because their flair for teamwork had triumphed once more.

So many Congo, Niger and even Nile boys did not stay to see Nile's last upsurge of form which rattled Zambezi so much that when they struggled home 21-18, the Zambezi players were so exhausted that they hardly realised that they had won the champion- ship for their house.

Friday, the last day of term began like a Saturday morning. There was full compound work and an inspection by the Principal. The Reverend Badger inspected as fastidiously as ever. Not for him the heady holiday mood of the students. As a result of this final inspection the Cleanliness Trophy went to Nile *House*.

The final assembly was held, as on
Saturdays, in the dining-hall. After the school
hymn and 'God be with you till we meet
again...', the Reverend Badger said farewell
prayers. Then with a broad fatherly grin, he
wished everyone 'Happy Holidays!' and got a
heart-warming response of the same
goodwill greeting.

All the business part of the end of term had
been completed the previous afternoon - the
examination results, the terminal reports, and
pocket money. All that was left now after the
warm exchange of greetings with The Badger
was for lorries to take students to the nearest
railway station or straight to their homes; for
bicycles to take home those whose homes were
nearer; and for those whose homes were within
walking distance to head for home on foot.

'Happy holidays, Willie!' Alexander Nwosu
greeted Wilson who was standing by his

luggage waiting for his father. 'I could not see you yesterday.' Then in a whisper, 'What was your exam result like?'

'Not too bad,' Wilson replied.

'What d'you mean by "not too bad"? Did you fail?' Alexander demanded angrily.

'No.'

'So you passed. Good show! What position did you take?' Alexander asked, his voice rising with excitement.

'I was all right,' Wilson answered vaguely.

'What do you mean by being all right? Stop kidding, Willie. If you really passed, why don't you tell me what position you took?'

'Well, first,' Wilson revealed.

'No!' Alexander shouted, gripping Wilson.

'So you don't like it?' Wilson asked, puzzled.

'Like it? I love it! Of course I do. It's wonderful. As I said earlier, you are the boy after my own heart. Congratulations, Willie my boy. Your days in St Mark's will now definitely be long.'

'Thank you, Alex.'

www.ingramcontent.com/pod-product-compliance
Lightning Source LLC
Chambersburg PA
CBHW060402310726
48976CB00003B/912